When, out of desperation, Bran Caspar takes a job in a women's designer shoe store, little does he know he's just entered a world of secret shoe fetishes and a string of cafés designed to cater to a man's every whim and secret obsessions. It's a world that turns out to be deadly but highly compelling, especially with a certain "maid" named Rick.

For Bran's best friend, Finn, the prospect of a new business is a pleasant distraction from his horrible breakup with his lover, Waldo. And speaking of which, where is Waldo? Right inside The Fetish Café, looking for more than a cup of coffee.

Will these best friends find happiness at the end of their shift, or will they, too, become victims of The Fetish Café?

This book has been previously published.

The Fetish Café
Copyright © 2019 A.J. Llewellyn and D.J. Manly
ISBN: 978-1-4874-2460-2
Cover art by Martine Jardin

Published by eXtasy Books Inc or
Devine Destinies, an imprint of eXtasy Books Inc

Look for us online at:
www.eXtasybooks.com or www.devinedestinies.com

The Fetish Café

BY

A.J. LLEWELLYN AND D.J. MANLY

DEDICATION

To our readers, with love . . .

Chapter One

"So what do you think?"

Bran Caspar glanced around the powder blue, silver, and white interior of the store, aptly named Winter, and tried to rustle up some enthusiasm for it. What a massive comedown after graduating from Harvard summa cum laude. He'd made the dean's list and had worked hard for all his accolades, not to mention the glowing references he'd been given during his multiple internships.

And yet, the best he could do three months after graduating was to get a part-time job in a shoe store.

A ladies' shoe store.

What he knew about ladies shoes wouldn't even fill, well . . . a lady's shoe.

But his new, prospective boss, Paul Winter, was kinda hot, and sixteen bucks an hour was almost double the minimum wage.

It's temporary. Everybody has to start somewhere. Never lose sight of that.

He gazed out of the gleaming bay windows at quaint, sunny Colorado Boulevard. Nestled in the heart of Old Town Pasadena in LA's eastern suburbs, the store radiated money. Actually, a lot more than that. Money, class, and taste.

He knew the dynamic, blond, frosty-blue-eyed, handsome Paul wanted an answer. The owner and designer of Winter was proud of his accomplishments and appeared to be passionate, no, *fanatical* about ladies shoes. He swept a casual hand around what he called his salon. Decorated with antique chaises and tiny sofas, each shoe displayed stood on a pedestal that looked like icicles.

"It's an unusually quiet day. I hope you'll be able to handle the stress."

"I can't wait to start," Bran lied. *This is only happening to me because my mom named me after some ancient Welsh king who got his head cut off. Oh, my God. Am I going to be one of those people who peaks in college?*

"This is one of the of the most successful businesses in Pasadena. I'm planning to open a second store on Montana Avenue, then possibly a third on Abbott Kinney. So you see, I'll need your help." The note of pride in Paul's voice was understandable.

I wonder how many languages he speaks. Did he give up his entire childhood to shoe leather?

He knew Paul wasn't lying because he'd read everything about the lucrative boutique before driving out here from Santa Monica to meet the guy.

The job of three days a week manager hadn't been advertised. Bran's mother was a huge Winter customer. She had her own shoe fetish and constantly posted her purchases on Facebook.

I must take a closer look at her shoes.

She'd sung her son's praises, begging Paul to give him a chance. And just this morning, she'd educated Bran about the finer brands in female foot couture. His brain swam with the names, colors, dimensions . . .

She'd even taken him to a warehouse out near the airport where Lady Gaga's archivist had lovingly put each and every last shoe, slipper, and boot the singer had ever worn into hermetically sealed storage.

He'd casually mentioned this to Paul, even remarking on the hand-stitched boots the designer Alexander McQueen had made for the diva before taking his own life.

"Is it true she has one of the original pairs of Dorothy's slippers from *The Wizard of Oz*?" Paul had been agog.

"Yes, but I wasn't allowed to touch them. Or even take photos."

Paul drooled. "I'd love to see her collection!" he enthused.

Bran had nodded, saying he would hook him up. As he looked over the sale items and their hefty, three-hundred dollar price tag, he wondered if his dad realized how much his mom spent on shoes.

And I bet hers weren't on the sales rack . . .

Bran wasn't into shoes so much. He was more of a Foot Locker type of guy. He owned Nike and Puma running shoes and a pair of black, leather slip-ons for formal events such as weddings and funerals.

He took a deep breath as he realized Paul still waited for his response.

"I love it," Bran said, but inside, he wept. He felt his dreams of being an entrepreneur crumbling beneath his feet. *I should be wearing better shoes, at least.*

He was well-educated and fluent in six languages. He now began to resent the hours, months, no, *years*, he'd spent studying Korean, Japanese, Mandarin, Bahasa Indonesia, Javanese, and of course, English.

It still rankled that he'd failed to score a huge job through an international recruitment firm requiring somebody who could speak both Bahasa Indonesia and Javanese. The job seemed like a dream. Quarter of a million dollars a year, with a guaranteed two-year minimum for a new computer firm in Jakarta.

Bran had been certain he'd get it. He didn't know anyone else with his qualification, let alone his language skills. He'd been so sure he'd land the job he'd begun planning how he'd live in Jakarta and sock away his income, investing in gold and other markets, and just hunker down for two years.

The recruiter had wined and dined Bran. He'd been impressed by his credentials and confided that he'd put Bran on the top of his list. Two weeks later, he learned from the same man that another interviewee had been deemed more appropriate because he had a few more after-school activities under his belt.

How? How was it possible? His mind still reeled over his spectacular flop. It hurt. Really hurt. The only way Bran could have squeezed one more course, one more bit of education into his daily itinerary, was to have given up sleeping completely.

He took a breath, inhaling the scent of new leather.

"Good," Paul said, unaware that Bran hadn't eaten and the sharp smells in the store made him a bit weak and dizzy. "Now, as I mentioned before, we get a lot of men coming in here for shoes. Is that a problem for you?"

Paul's gaze became intense. One might say he looked downright worried.

Bran looked at him, puzzled. "No, not at all." Why should it? His dad frequently accompanied his mom on shopping expeditions. He'd always assumed it was because they were still passionately in love after all these years—and they were—but he'd started to realize it was to curb her outrageous spending habits.

"By the way, the book *Shoes: A History from Sandals to Sneakers* is required reading," Paul said. "You can pick up a copy on Amazon. I expect you to do that today."

Today? But I don't even have money for food! I've been eating peanut butter sandwiches for the last six days!

"I'm curious to get your opinion once you start reading," Paul said. "I wonder if you'll agree that Cinderella is a story of fetishism and hegemony."

Bran stared at him. *Hegemony? Is this guy kidding me right now? He thinks Cinderella is a story about dominance and control? And what kind of fetish is he talking about? Man, I think he might be a genuine fruitcake.*

He didn't have time to ponder these thoughts. Paul seemed to believe that Bran was a shoe expert and if he was going to keep this job he needed to bone up on footwear. Fast.

Paul shook his hand with surprising strength. "You can start tomorrow."

"Okay, great."

"Be here at nine. We don't open until ten, but I need to show you how everything works. The computers, stock room. I'll spend your first day with you, teaching you the ropes. We do custom orders. Oh." Paul snapped his fingers and flashed a whiter shade of pale. "I'll need you to fill out a non-disclosure form. It's fairly lengthy, but I know your father's an attorney, so I don't mind you having him look it over. It's imperative that all my employees sign an agreement promising never to write a tweet, a Facebook post, a blog . . . anything, about what they see here."

Bran stared at him. *Now I know he's a fruitcake.*

The door opened, and Paul's head turned. "God. She's a day early," he muttered, barely audible.

Bran stared at the figure before him. It was his favorite pop singer, Brenda Bright, and she rushed in on massively high heels. Bran's mom had told him six-inch high heels were all the rage now, but the singer tottered so badly she fell into Paul's waiting arms.

They laughed at one another, and after swapping numerous air kisses, Brenda's impish gaze fell on Bran.

"And who's this cutie pie?"

Paul quickly introduced them. Brenda didn't take her ruby-red nails off Paul's arm for a second. She blew a kiss at Bran, then turned, beckoning her head over her shoulder. A tall, dark figure emerged from a stretch limo Bran hadn't noticed parked out front. He almost swallowed his tongue when rap singer Jack Tappin strolled into the store. From everything Bran had read about the couple, they were a real fuck and fight team. They raged against each other on Twitter and Instagram, but couldn't stay apart for long.

The latest scuttlebutt was that he'd hit her, or was it the other way around? They were supposedly separated.

Wait until I tell Finn!

Bran couldn't believe it when Paul introduced him to Jack, and the singer shook Bran's hand. The way he made direct eye contact with Bran as he said, "Nice to meet you, Bran," had Bran swooning. He could see why Brenda couldn't stay away from the guy. He was even sexier in person than on TV.

He stood back and watched Paul handle Brenda as though she were a priceless, fragile piece of porcelain. He seated her on a chaise, and Jack flopped beside her.

For one horrible moment, as Paul vanished to the back of the store, Bran thought he might be required to make conversation with the couple, but they were busy kissing. Brenda held up her cell phone and took a selfie as Jack nuzzled her creamy throat.

A few seconds later, Paul was back with a satin-colored box, tape measure tossed around his neck.

"Can I get you a coffee? Champagne?" he asked his customers.

"Champagne," they said in unison. Bran couldn't speak as Paul disappeared behind a corner bar Bran hadn't noticed before because it blended so well with the silvery-white walls.

"Lock the front door, please, Bran," Paul instructed. "And please put the 'Back in ten minutes sign' on it."

Paul obeyed his boss's instructions, intrigued to see that the front door's glass panels had been frosted with huge W's and were hard to see through. He returned just as Paul handed the singers flute glasses of Tattinger.

Bran noticed that Paul didn't imbibe, and he didn't offer

Bran a glass either. He propped himself on a low chair, a footstool made to look like an icicle in front of him.

To Bran's shock, it was Jack who put his feet on the stool. He hoped he didn't gasp or emit any other sounds as Bran rolled stocking socks over Paul's feet.

The two singers beamed down at Jack's tootsies. Brenda reached out and stroked the top of Jack's left foot as Paul opened his satin box and withdrew a pair of strappy black sandals with super-high heels and gold embellishments. The embellishments read the letter B.

Paul slipped them onto Jack's feet. The singer looked thrilled, as did Brenda, who cooed, "He's mine, all mine."

"Are they comfortable?" Paul asked Jack, who immediately got to his feet and walked around.

Bran didn't know where to look. He was embarrassed to see a manly, sexy guy in women's high heels.

"Perfect," Jack said, his voice breathless. "When will you have the diamonds put on the straps?"

"Tomorrow. Georg" — he pronounced it Gay-yorg — "will be here at noon."

"Perfect," Jack said again. He walked around, admiring himself in the mirrors that sprang out from strategically hidden wall panels. Bran had to admit the man had shapely calves. But why, oh why, did he want to wear women's shoes?

Bran said nothing as Jack returned to the chaise and Paul fussed with the straps and clasp on the shoes.

"Bran saw Lady Gaga's Dorothy shoes this morning," Paul told his customers.

Brenda stared at Bran. "Is that true? I heard they were given to her as a birthday present a few years ago."

Bran nodded. "I heard the same thing."

"Do you know where the shoes came from? I'd love to get a pair for Brenda," Jack said.

She put her hands around her lover's arm and squeezed. "You're so sweet!"

"I don't, I'm sorry."

"He went to visit Lady Gaga's costume archives." Paul sat up straighter, turning his eager gaze on Bran. "Oh, Bran, do you think you could ask your friend to let us all see her work?"

"Oh, yes." Brenda enthused. "I've heard about her. She's done heaps of people's archives. Maybe she could do mine. Here's my card. Call me anytime. I never sleep."

That's where I went wrong. Bran took the card, gave her a smile and said, "I'll be in touch." He glanced at the numbers. *I have all of her details. My God! Finn's gonna croak!*

The vibes in the store were very friendly by the time the singers left.

"You're going to work well here," Paul said. "Since I made you work, how about I treat you to lunch?"

Bran's rumbling stomach leaped at the suggestion of a free meal, but he'd told his best friend, Finn Duchesne, that he'd meet him at Starbucks at noon and give him the news. Finn had been his friend since they'd met at Harvard. They'd fought off a mutual attraction in favor of concentrating on school and future success, only now, both men were having a hard time finding work, and Finn had a boyfriend. It upset Bran tremendously, not that he'd ever let on.

"Having a hard time deciding if you want to have lunch with me?" Paul asked.

"No. I'd love to have lunch with you, but I told my friend I'd meet him for coffee."

Paul waved a hand in that expansive way of his. "Call him, have him meet us. There's a wonderful restaurant a few doors down. I hope you'll like it."

Two hours later, Bran had eaten the best meal he'd had in months. He also had a job, and so, thanks to Bran, did Finn.

The two college stars would split the shifts between them as managers of Winter, allowing the celebrated designer more time to work on his custom pieces. Paul was such a cool guy, Bran was already developing a crush on him.

Finn wasn't so sure. "There's something off about him," he said as they swam in Finn's parents' pool later that day. They'd given up their Gold's Gym memberships until their cash flow situation resolved itself. They worked out in the Duchesne family's home gym and swam laps in the pool.

"I wouldn't get too close to him if I were you," Finn said, lolling against the steps in the shallow end.

"What do you mean, off?" Bran couldn't help bristling at Finn's criticism. He hoisted himself out of the pool and grabbed a towel. He dried himself with rough, rapid movements. Bran hadn't particularly liked Finn's boyfriend, Waldo, when he'd met him, but he'd refrained from saying so. Waldo was so fond of disappearing on Finn, their mutual friends often cracked, "Where's Waldo?"

"I don't know." Finn climbed out of the pool and joined Bran on the sun deck. "There's something a little bit . . . shady about it. I can't put my finger on it."

Bran said nothing. He let out a sigh. "I should be in Jakarta."

"No, B. I would have missed you."

Bran smiled. "I would have missed you, too." He and Finn had dark hair, and, Bran liked to think, good looks, but Finn had an extra sparkle Bran thought of as superstar quality. They'd been on every debating team possible at college and frequently argued about small points. It drove people around them nuts, but they thrived on the banter. Right now, however, Bran didn't like it so much.

And then, to add to his misery, Waldo arrived, striding across the terrace toward them. Waldo sucked the air out of any room just by entering it.

"Gotta go," Bran said. The last thing he wanted was a debate with both Finn and his lover.

"Stay, B," Finn said.

"Naw. I'm gonna get going." He hadn't told Finn that he'd received a text message from Paul Winter inviting him to drinks. He scuttled out of the side gate as fast as his legs could carry him.

In his car, he texted Paul back. They exchanged several messages, the last one from Paul saying, *You don't live far from me. I'll pick you up at eight.*

To his dismay, Paul was waiting out front for him when he got to his apartment on Euclid.

Paul gave him a finger wave and got out of his BMW. It took Bran a moment to absorb the fact that the designer was driving a 2014 M6. The vehicle had a price tag of over a hundred thousand dollars. Dang. There was money in shoe fetishes, for sure.

He rushed into his apartment, Paul on his heel. He had no time to shower but threw on fresh jeans and an A and F shirt. He put on his black loafers, surprised when Paul nodded his approval.

"So European," he said.

They left the apartment and drove off to downtown LA, an area Bran did his best to spend as little time in as possible. Where the hell were they going?

The BMW got a lot of admirers as they zipped across lanes on the Hollywood Freeway.

Paul began to burble about shoes. "You will find you become passionate about them once you handle them all day long," he said.

I don't think so. Bran began to revise his notions of a Paul Winter crush.

"What did you think of the sandals I made for Jack?"

"Very interesting," Bran said. "I've never seen anything quite like them."

"Ah, that's because they're modeled on an ancient pair of sandals as worn by prostitutes in Pompeii."

Startled, Bran asked, "Really?"

"Really. I read about them in the book you're going to read."

Bran winced. He'd forgotten to order the damned thing.

"Back in Pompeii and ancient Greece, women wore strappy sandals as a sign of belonging to the men in their lives."

Bran recalled now the moment Brenda had said, *"He's mine, all mine,"* about Jack. So basically, Jack was her whore.

"How much would shoes like that cost the client?" Bran blurted.

"Well . . ." Paul pulled a face. "Usually, the record label or studio pays so they're a little looser with the purse strings, but since Brenda ordered them herself, she's only paying eighty-five thousand dollars."

Only? My God! There's a gold mine here! Bran listened and learned and realized that Paul Winter was making a killing. And then some.

They pulled up outside a café that seemed closed by the looks of things. Stenciled in gold across the windows were the words *The Maid Café.*

A valet driver stepped out of the shadows and took possession of the vehicle. Bran felt sheer anxiety at the prospect of being on South Figueroa in the encroaching dark. Apart from the café, nothing else seemed to be on the street except a few derelicts sleeping against garbage bins.

Paul opened a gold-handled door, and they walked inside.

Bran was astonished to see the place jumping with activity. He didn't know where to look first. He'd never seen so many gorgeous young women in one place in his entire life, and LA was a city that pumped them out like gusts of smog. Almost all were Asian and dressed like French maids. They tittered as they whirled around the packed eatery delivering laden trays of food and drink.

Wow. Bran had just realized some of the maids were men. Gorgeous men. He thought about Jack and the strappy shoes. He sensed a trend here. Some of the maids wore animals ears, and many got tips shoved into interior pockets of their tiny aprons.

"Thank you!" the maids chorused, dancing around in their high heels.

"Welcome home, Master Paul!" a pretty, delicate-looking young Japanese woman said, handing him a warm, wet, hand towel. As Paul introduced Mimi to Bran, she gave him a sweet, deep curtsey and, from that position, handed Bran his own towel. Now, this was service.

From the corner of his eye, he caught a glimpse of a glamorous-looking young man with copper hair and an unusual nose. Everything about him seemed graceful and cat-like. He turned haunting, dark eyes on Bran as if taking his measure, and then moving on to deliver food to a table.

Frantic Japanese music streamed out from somewhere. Pink and blue bubbles burst out of little holes in the walls and floated lazily toward the ceiling.

The food looked great and smelled fantastic, but Paul Winter commanded immediate attention, from patrons and maids alike. A few people rushed over and kissed him. He introduced Bran to each person who came his way.

There was a moment when Bran knew he could and *should* cut bait and run, or plunge into the heady, hectic world of fetishism.

He took a deep breath and shook hands with each person, practicing his best business behavior. He filed away names in his mind, associating each with something he could remember easily with which to associate them. He talked with ease, moving fluently between Korean, Chinese, and English, feeling the weight of Paul's appraising gaze on him.

"I can tell by your facial expression you've never been to one of these before," Paul said, taking Bran by the elbow and steering him to a secluded table.

"You mean there's more?" Bran shouted above the noise.

"Oh, yes." As they sat in the quiet corner far from the main action, Paul yawned and stretched. "These maid cafés started twelve years ago in Tokyo. Now they've branched out, and they're all over the world, but they're not exactly family friendly. They do no publicity and get by on word of mouth."

Bran's gaze flicked from a man in a business suit massaging a maid's dainty feet to a male maid gently kissing a leather-clad biker's beard as he laughed. Family friendly? Probably not. He grinned, sensing the happy, yet kinky vibes in the joint. As he sat opposite Paul, he took it all in.

Maids served food kneeling on the floor. They remained by their customers' sides, stirring their coffee, laughing at their jokes. A few massaged their clients' shoulders, played computer games, or drew pictures with them. Everything was fun and flirty skirting the edge of romantic danger.

"The Maid Cafés were originally created to serve *otaku*." Paul gave a significant pause. "You know what they are?"

"Yes. They're people who have fetishes for certain characters in anime or manga."

"Right. So these young lovelies dress as some of the famous characters." Paul leaned close. "See the beautiful copper-haired boy over there?" He gestured toward the bar. Bran nodded. Yes, he'd noticed that spectacular specimen. "They say he's had his nose surgically altered to look like a cat."

"Really?" For some reason, Bran doubted it. He had a feeling the maid was a clever performer.

"They say those are genuine leopard whiskers. He gets

new ones implanted when the old ones break off."

Eeew! No way. That has to be a gimmick.

"He's the most popular maid here," Paul said. By his tone, Bran could tell Paul had a soft spot for the guy.

Always the bridesmaid . . .

"You like *omurice*?" Paul asked. "I can order one for us to share."

"Sure." Bran had never tasted one. How bad could it be? Paul flirted outrageously with the copper-haired maid, whose eyes lit up at the fifty-dollar bill Paul waved in his direction.

He scooted over, meowing, and mauling Paul in an affectionate, kittenish way. It was oddly seductive to see the way the maid pampered Paul in a suggestive, yet not crass way. Paul was a mess. He clearly adored the guy.

"Paul, meet my darling Copper." Another fifty disappeared into Copper's apron pocket.

Bran realized the café maids treated their clients as though they were the masters, or in the case of two women he spotted, mistresses, coming home from a long day at work. A couple of men were getting shaves in one section, with old-fashioned, hand-held razors. Another one was receiving a scalp massage a few chairs down.

Bran waited as Copper and Paul chit-chatted, sharing some private joke. *Geez, this is like going out for a meal with Finn and Waldo. Maybe I should have bought that book about shoes. That would keep me occupied.*

A few minutes later, Paul ordered coffees and iced water for them both, and the famous omurice. When it arrived, it turned out to be a thin omelet stuffed with fragrant fried rice, topped with what looked like ketchup. It was absolutely delicious.

Copper was attentive and kind, attending to their every need. He somehow knew that Bran's omelet needed a little salt and seasoned it for him. It was excellent service, and beyond.

"I provide shoes for the maids," Paul said between bites, as Copper sashayed away to find them "some yummy dessert" as Paul commanded him. Copper returned with what he said was shave ice but was a frothy, icy confection containing tons of fresh fruit layered with shave ice, cream, and ice cream laced with a tangy passionfruit sauce.

Copper sat beside Paul, spoon feeding him. He smiled when he caught Bran's bereft expression. "I know. Finishing it is heart-breaking, isn't it? It's my favorite thing on the menu."

Bran leaned back. Whoever had designed the place had come up with a brilliant idea. He wondered if he and Finn could find the investors, if they could come up with their own fetish café, delivering the same sort of services, but a whole lot more. As in, actual sex.

He kept thinking about this as Paul and Copper played some computer game. Paul received a text message that made him stiffen, and suddenly, their fun time was over.

Paul paid their check, leaving a massive tip.

"Thank you for coming, Master," Copper said, but his gaze remained on Bran as he said the words.

"Thank you, Copper." Bran happily exchanged kisses on both sides of his face with Copper, who repeated the gesture with Paul.

"Come back and see me, soon, Master," Copper said, his tone low and seductive.

By the time the car arrived out front, Paul was in a snit. "He likes you more than me."

"No, no. He was trying to be nice to me to impress you."

"You think so?" Paul's eyes lit up again.

No, I don't. All I know is, I want to go back to that place. I want to see that man.

Paul dropped him at home. "Sorry, but I have a meeting."

"I understand." *What kind of meeting does a person have late at night?* Bran lifted a hand and said, "Thank you for a great evening. See you tomorrow."

He could hardly sleep. He paced his living room floor and called Finn, but didn't leave any messages. He wanted to talk to his friend in person. Finn was back home by midnight and called him, intrigued with the story Bran told him.

"I think we could talk Paul into opening a fetish café. We'll cater to people who want to dress up. It wouldn't just be the maids. We could have secret rooms, secret rendezvous. I'd love to hire the maid I met tonight, Copper. He must have cleared five hundred bucks in tips alone from Paul tonight."

"We could always take jobs there ourselves," Finn suggested. "I mean, for that money I'd be game."

"But I wouldn't. I want to be a boss, not a worker."

"Fair enough. When do I get to check out this place?"

"How about tomorrow, after I finish work?"

"You have yourself a date, Master," Finn said, ending their call.

The next day at work, Paul had a ton of orders to fulfill but was patient and helpful with Bran. They worked from nine in the morning until eight o'clock that night. It was a long day, but challenging and rewarding. Paul had experienced a lot in his twenty-nine years and had a clear idea of his brand, and what he wanted to achieve with it.

Over the next two weeks, he talked a lot to Bran and Finn about his life. The only rough moments were the times Paul received odd phone calls that made him tense. Finn had seen this, too. As he and Bran began to spend all their evenings at The Maid Café, they pondered what the problem could be.

"Yakuza," Finn finally said one evening. "I saw a black car pull up and two Japanese guys got out. He didn't seem to realize I was behind the bar washing out some champagne glasses. He gave those dudes a lot of cash. It was the only time I ever saw him look nervous. He's usually so confident, so cool."

It was true. Bran thought about this as the days went on. Paul seemed more and more nervous, falling into silent lapses in the middle of discussions about shoe samples for different department stores, or items he was donating for gala benefits.

One evening, as he and Paul were working late to complete an order of his and her lace-up ankle boots for a celebrity couple, a black car pulled up out front.

"Oh, shit. Hide," Paul said and started to sweat.

Bran had nowhere to go and didn't want to leave his boss alone when he was so pale and shaky. The door opened.

"Go." Paul's face had turned chalk white, his voice a frightened whisper that made Bran shiver.

A deep male voice wished Paul a good evening as Bran slid to the floor, and unseen, hid behind the ice-blue bar.

"What do you want, Mr. Takashi?" Paul sounded strange. Not just frightened, but . . . defeated.

"I want money. Isn't that what I always want?"

"I paid my key money already this week."

"But it's not enough. Two full-time employees—"

"Part-time. Each one works three days a week."

"I want double what you've been giving me."

"But I can't. I simply can't."

Bran hoped his own mounting terror didn't make him do something stupid.

"Where is the one who was here helping you?" the angry Japanese man asked.

"He's gone home. I sent him away just before you came."

"Check the storeroom," the man said.

Bran heard footsteps receding, then returning again. "Empty," a second man said.

"So we're all alone?" the first man asked.

"Yes, yes," Paul said. "All alone."

Two shots that sounded weird rang out. Bran bit his lip to stifle a scream.

A long silence ensued, and Bran waited. And waited. The front door opened and closed again, but still, he waited.

Total panic engulfed him, but he was worried about his boss. He crawled out to find Paul on the floor, blood floating from his body like the wings of a butterfly.

God, he was still alive. "Don't call the police," Paul whispered. "Please. Let me die. Take my shoes. Take my money. Take it all. Don't let them get it. There's a key to my car in the register. I've stashed all my cash in . . . in . . ." He gasped. "They'll be back in a moment. Money's in the car. Hidden. Fuck it hurts to get shot. Open your café. Good-bye, Bran. Good—"

With that last word, he was gone.

Bran freaked out. His boss, his friend, the one man who'd given him a chance, was gone. Could he take his money and run?

He got to his feet. He had no time. He took the key to the BMW, the appointment book, as many boxes of shoes as would fit into Paul's vehicle, and drove off. He didn't think about the fact that his own car was still parked on Colorado Street.

Bran pulled over to the curb and called Finn. Damn him. As usual, Bran went to voice mail. He left a message, still not able to process the fact that he and Finn now had money. They could live their dream. Could they really open a fetish café? And where was the money hidden?

He'd have to take the car apart and hunt for it all.

Poor Paul. *Key money.* He knew what that meant. He'd been leaned on, way too heavily, and played with the big boys.

Fate had dealt him a very rough hand.

What if they come after me?

We need to leave town.

Me, Finn. Waldo, if we have to. And Copper. We need Copper. We can reinvent ourselves. We can follow our hearts. We'll follow Paul's.

As he turned down Colorado Boulevard, he didn't look back.

It housed too many broken dreams.

CHAPTER TWO

When Bran called Finn to tell him he was coming over, he could hardly make out what Finn was trying to say. He was blubbering something in between sobs. "Finn, for Christ's sakes," Bran snapped, "I can't make out a damned word you're saying. You're loaded. What's going on?"

Finn started to blubber again, and Bran said, "Stop. You can tell me when I get there. We gotta talk. Open your garage door."

"Why?"

"Just because. Do it." *Damn it,* Bran thought as he hung up, of all the times for Finn to be sloshed.

Finn lived in an upscale part of LA near Lacy Park, in a huge house with six bedrooms. His parents had died in a car crash when Finn was a teenager. He'd been brought up by his aunt in Beverly Hills but inherited the house when he was twenty-one. Most of what he had was wrapped up in the house, so he really did need to make money.

The garage was open when Bran got there, and he drove directly in. Finn stood there waiting for him, or rather, he tottered there, half-drunk bottle of something lethal in his hand.

"Okay," Bran said, "what happened?" He opened the car door but stayed inside, searching the glove compartment. *No. Paul wouldn't have made it that easy.*

"What's going on?" Finn demanded. He leaned down into the car and just about fell over. And his breath was enough to make Bran fall over.

"Jesus, Finn." Bran got out of the car and reached out to steady his friend. "What's going on with you?"

"Waldo left me. I can't find him."

Bran began to snigger. "Are you kidding me?" He was suddenly reminded of that stupid game. Didn't you have to find Waldo or something?

"Why are you laughing?" Finn bellowed. "He's left me."

Bran's eyes widened. "Left you?"

Finn lowered his head.

"Oh no. This can't be happening. Finn, listen to me," Bran put his hands on Finn's shoulders. "You need to sober up. I have something to tell you . . . something big."

"What?" Finn rubbed his eyes.

"First, upstairs and sleep it off." Bran pushed Finn upstairs and toward the bedroom. "Bed, sleep, now!"

"Tell me what's . . ." Finn muttered as they walked inside. Finn stumbled a couple of times climbing upstairs. In his bedroom, Bran could see it was disheveled.

Man, he really is upset. This isn't like him at all.

"No, you won't hear me. You're about to pass out. And give me that!" He took the rest of the booze. "Vodka?" He read the label. He put it on the bureau and pulled the blankets down on Finn's bed. A few minutes later, Finn had conked out on top of it.

Bran picked up what was left of the Vodka and went back to the garage. He took a healthy swig, just realizing how shaken he was. He leaned against the wall and closed his eyes, picturing poor Paul and all that blood. He took another gulp then went to work. He had to find that money.

An hour later he had it after cutting open the lining of the trunk that had been most skillfully glued together again. When he pulled up the corner, he let out a gasp. Thousand dollar bills were scattered under that lining, at least five hundred of them or more. He didn't count them. He just gathered them all together then went upstairs. He tucked them into a plastic bag and conked out on Finn's sofa.

When he opened his eyes, Finn sat slumped in a chair across from where he was sleeping, with an icepack on his head and a mug of coffee in his hand.

Bran reared up on his elbow. "Don't answer the door. You didn't, did you?"

"No," he replied. He sounded as if he was in pain when he spoke. "Why so paranoid?"

"Paul is dead." Bran sat up on the sofa.

Finn lowered the ice pack and looked at him. "What did you say?"

"He was murdered. I was in the store. I think he was into the mob."

"Damn. The police—"

"No. I didn't call the police. Listen, he told me to take his car and . . . look." Bran pulled out the plastic bag from under the cushion. "Money."

"Bran, you gotta tell the cops." Finn stared agog at all the money.

"I'll deal with it, I promise." He looked around. "I want to start a café, a fetish café, a real one."

"You've lost your mind!"

"No, I haven't. We can cater to the richest people. We can get Copper to help us with contacts."

"Who?"

"The cat guy who was working at The Maid Café, Copper. He'd come in with us I think."

"Do you know how to find him?"

"Sure."

"Bran, you need to tell the cops you saw the murderer."

Bran sighed. "I didn't actually see him, but you're right. I was an ear witness, as opposed to an eye witness. His name is Takashi. Maybe I have seen him before. Some Asian guys have been around there before when you and I have been there, demanding money."

"That's true," Finn said.

"But I can't put a face to the name." Bran tried to think. He recounted the entire episode to Finn, who stared at him in shock. "I'll contact the cops, I promise."

"Where would this club be?"

"Here."

"*Here*? As in, this house?"

"It's perfect. Listen, if Copper can give us his contacts, word will spread. It will be by invitation only, exclusive clientele. Whatever their fantasy, we will provide, along with good coffee and succulent, sinful desserts. We can do this."

Finn looked shell-shocked.

"Now, what happened between you and Waldo?"

"He's been stepping out on me with another guy. He told me today, said he wanted to go away with this guy."

"I'm sorry. But . . . well fuck him, Finn. Are you with me on this thing? You provide the setting, and I'll pay to renovate it. Copper can provide the contacts. We'll be rich."

Finn hesitated for a second then nodded. "What the hell! I never did know what to do with all this space anyway."

Bran began to think his degree in business from Harvard was about to pay off big time. He felt bad about Paul, but he didn't intend on making the same mistakes.

A stop a day later at The Maid Café found the place greatly changed. Bran and Finn walked in to find it half empty. The waiters and waitresses were standing around dressed quite simply, and Bran spotted the one he knew as Copper pouring coffee behind the counter. There were no whiskers implanted in his face, as Paul had suggested, and he wore jeans and a sweatshirt.

Bran and Finn walked over to the counter and Copper, after handing over a cup of java to one of the waitresses, noticed them there. "Well, hello." He smiled at Bran and then nodded politely at Finn.

Bran wasted no time. "What's your real name?"

"I beg your pardon?"

"You're not really called Copper."

"No." He shook his head. "Listen, things have changed. We have some sad news. The café is to be closed down. The police have been here. Paul is . . . was, one of the owners and . . . well, he was murdered."

"I know," Bran said. Copper seemed surprised but said nothing as Bran went on. "I . . . I'm so sorry. I came to here to offer you a job." Damn, he was cute.

"Doing what? The shoe store is closed, too."

"Listen, when do you get off?" Finn interjected. Maybe he noticed how Bran couldn't stop staring at this guy, and it seemed mutual.

Copper checked his watch. "In an hour."

"We'll wait," Bran said.

"Sorry, I can't offer you anything but coffee and pastries."

"Sounds good, whatever you've got," Bran said. "We'll get a table."

Copper nodded.

Finn leaned over to Bran after they sat at a corner table. "Whoa, there was some heat being exchanged there."

"He's cute, isn't he?" Bran grinned.

"Yeah. But will he be into it?" Finn fiddled with a napkin.

"We have a sound business plan, and we have the place. If I'm correct, Copper is going to help to get us started. Did you get confirmation from the construction crew?"

"Yeah. They'll be there tomorrow morning. They have the plans. We'll have our private quarters, then the guest rooms as well as the café section. We can have entertainment there along with the refreshments."

"Perfect. I like the way you're thinking now." Bran

slapped Finn on the back. He looked at Copper as he approached with a tray of coffee and several *mille-feuille*, otherwise known as Napoleons. "Just perfect."

Finn shook his head as Copper emptied the tray.

"So," Bran looked up at him, "what is your name?"

"Rick Burns."

"Rick," Bran repeated. "Nice."

"Thanks. I'll join you soon." He smiled.

Bran smiled back.

"Oh brother," Finn muttered.

"Just because you are boyfriendless," Bran accused.

Finn sighed. "Waldo was a dickhead."

"I told you that."

"Never mind."

They drank their coffee and ate the pastries. Really nice. Bran loved custard, but Finn was the one with the sweet tooth. He ended up eating the tops, which were the icing sugar and dark chocolate swirls and trading in his custard with Bran.

They were finishing up when Rick picked up a chair, turned it around and sat at their table.

"So, shoot," he said. He sure was different from the cat he was doing the last time Bran saw him. He liked both actually.

Finn began. "You need a job. We have an idea, and we're willing to cut you in. We need you to be our liaison person."

"What kind of an idea are we talking about?" He lifted an eyebrow.

Bran leaned forward. "A fetish club, clandestine, by invite only. It would be a café too . . . we'd serve drinks, coffee, and desserts. "

"You want to make it like The Maid?" Rick asked.

"Not exactly," Finn lowered his voice. "We want to cater to every fetish."

"Excluding extreme S & M and anything that involves underage participants," Rick added.

Rick sat back for a minute.

"Do you have customers that might be interested, customers who want privacy and have loads of disposable income?" Finn added.

Rick shot forward in his chair. "Yes," he said. "The demand is there. And I know people who know people. I can fill your club."

Bran and Finn beamed.

"You need the right employees," Rick pointed out.

Finn winked. "I want in. Bran wants to manage. What about you?"

"Please say you'll participate," Bran urged. "You'll get to choose your clients, and of course we'll take no profit off the top. You keep it all as a partner."

Rick beamed. "Sounds great. Give me a few days to get the word out, and set up a new phone number where clients can call. How long before we're up and running?"

Bran looked at Finn.

"Two to three weeks," Finn replied.

"We could have an open house," Bran said. "It would be just drinks and a chance for interested parties to check us out."

"What about a membership?" Finn asked.

"That's a great idea." Rick nodded. "Exclusive members will bring special guests and so on."

"We need to decide on prices and create some sort of surveys to find out what our clients want," Finn suggested.

"Rick," Bran asked, "do you also know people who'd want to work for us?"

"I think I could rustle up a few." He nodded.

"Perfect," Finn said.

"We want this all on the up and up between us," Bran

said. "So we'll draw up a partnership agreement. We split everything three ways, including expenses. If we cater to a client on our own, however, we keep all of it. Any idea about what we should charge?"

"Rick?" Finn looked at him. "Any suggestions?"

"Let me give it some thought," he said.

"Maybe you should come back and see the place," Bran mentioned. "You can look over the plans and see if there are any changes you'd like to make before the construction crew gets to Finn's place tomorrow."

Finn gave Bran a look. Bran ignored it.

"Oh, the club is in your house?" Rick asked Finn.

"Well, it . . . yes." Finn grinned. "It's near Lacy Park, last house on the street, really quiet."

"Perfect," Rick said. "Just perfect."

Finn didn't make himself scarce like Bran thought he would. Instead, he followed Bran and Rick around the house like a puppy dog. Rick really liked how the house was to be divided. He made a suggestion or two about where the bar should be located and also the bathroom. Bran made a note for the construction company.

"There's so much to do," Bran added. "We need to choose the décor for the bedrooms. What do you think, by color?"

Rick pursed his lips. "Well, since the clients will mostly be men, nothing too frilly. Classy, satin sheets, black, and different colored duvets with matching cushions. Cushions come in handy."

Bran smiled. He could think of things to do with cushions at the moment, like propping one under Rick's cute little bubble butt.

"Bran." Finn nudged him.

"Yeah?"

"Rick was asking about the basement."

"Oh yes." Bran nodded. "We don't want to make it too house of horrors, do we?"

"No," Rick said, "but I know a guy who's an expert in that stuff. He can get you the right equipment."

"Would he work here?" Bran asked.

"As a consultant."

"Good," Finn said. "We want to do things safely if we get clients requesting that sort of thing. We'll hire him, then?"

The two other men nodded.

Bran looked at Finn. *Please go out and do something.* Finn wasn't budging. Bran found himself bidding Rick goodnight at the front door. Damn. He didn't even get a kiss, let alone a fuck.

When Bran closed the door, he was prepared to give Finn shit. The television was blaring. They walked into the living room. Finn turned to him. "Bran, you gotta come and see this."

There on the television news was a picture of Paul. The next picture was of two Asian men. "They caught the killers," Finn looked at him. "This is great. You won't have to even go to the police."

Bran sank down on the sofa. It looked like things were really looking up. "That's great," he said.

Finn turned off the television. "I need to be up early, and so do you."

"Yeah . . . well . . ." Bran stood. "First, before you go, why couldn't you have left Rick and me alone for a bit tonight?"

"Because you wanted to fuck him."

"Yeah and so?"

"No yeah and so. We're business partners. I don't think we should be fucking each other."

"Is that a rule?"

"Yeah. I think it is."

"Damn. I don't like it."

"Tough titties." Finn grinned at him. "Night, partner."

Bran groaned and fell on the sofa.

The next few weeks were challenging to say the least. While Rick worked on hiring staff and sending out personal invites to former clients of The Maid Café and their friends, Bran and Finn made sure the construction company completed the work as laid out, the bar was stocked, the bedrooms and playroom downstairs was just right. They consulted with Rick's S and M person, a guy named Silas that looked like Bran's grade six gym teacher, and went over their surveys at least a hundred times making sure they didn't leave anything out.

"The category of *other* should compensate," Finn told Bran as they sat in the café part of the house, formerly Finn's living room. "We can cater to most kinds of kink."

"Yeah, but anything really weird like sex with live farm animals and out they go," Bran said.

Finn chuckled. "We won't have any clients."

"Rick called earlier. We have a guest list of over sixteen men. All of them rich, all of them wanting to remain anonymous."

Finn nodded. "The staff is ready. Rick said he'd make sure they were dressed appropriately or . . ." Finn grinned. "Not appropriately."

"The pastries arrive tomorrow at noon, gooey and delicious," Bran mentioned. "We're really doing this. Are you excited?"

"I am," Finn said, "but I'm curious to see if these rich guys will be willing to pay what we've set down as a membership fee?"

"Rick says they will," Bran replied.

"This is great. Bran, I do think this idea of yours borders on brilliance."

Bran held up a hand. "Let's ah . . . wait until tomorrow night, shall we before we declare it a success? I'd like to linger on the side of caution for a while."

"Fair enough."

They were sitting side by side on the sofa. Finn reached over and touched Bran's hand then leaned in and kissed him full on the lips.

Bran was stunned for a second.

Finn backed away, looking equally shell-shocked. "Sorry, I . . . I guess I got overcome by the moment."

"It's okay."

Suddenly they looked up, and Rick stood there. He was smiling. "Twenty. We got twenty for tomorrow night," he told them. "Hope we got enough donuts."

The three of them laughed.

The phone rang, and Finn went to answer it.

Bran met Rick's eyes. "You've done an incredible job."

"Thanks." He came closer.

"Are you intending on doing your cat routine?" Bran felt a little weak looking at Rick.

Rick came and sat beside him. "Maybe. I have a client coming who likes that sort of thing. Do you like it?"

Bran nodded.

Rick placed a hand on Bran's thigh. Their eyes met. *Oh boy*, Bran thought. *What's this?*

"You have beautiful eyes," Rick said softly.

"Thanks. You have . . ." He trailed off as Rick's hand slid higher.

"Yes?" he asked.

"Everything. Everything about you is . . ." Bran snaked his hand up around back of Rick's neck and pulled him forward. Their lips met, hot and electric, oh yeah. "I want to fuck you so bad," Bran groaned against his mouth.

Rick reared back. "What's stoppin' you?" His chest was

heaving.

"Finn says we . . . well we can't . . . we're partners and . . ."

"Fuck what Finn says." He sniggered. "He can join us if he wants."

Bran's eyelids flew open. Wow, a threesome with Rick and Finn. Um, that sounded nice.

"I bet he would if we asked," Rick suggested, his gaze going to the tent in Bran's pants.

"I don't know . . ." Bran said hesitantly.

Rick grabbed his hand and pulled him to his feet. "Let's ask him, shall we?"

Finn met them in the hallway. He looked perturbed about something.

"What is it?" Bran asked.

"It was Waldo."

"Oh," Bran looked at Rick. "His ex." He flicked his gaze back to Finn. "Are you all right?"

"Fine." He beamed. "I told him to go fuck himself."

Rick went into action. He walked over to Finn and placed a hand on his arm. "That's good."

"It is? Why?" Finn blinked.

"Because Bran and I"—Rick looked at Bran, who came closer—"would like to know if you would like to join us for a different kind of fucking."

"Will it feel as good as me telling Waldo to fuck himself?" Finn lifted an eyebrow.

"Better," Bran said, meeting his gaze.

Finn nodded. "Lead the way."

"What about your rule?"

"Fuck the rules, fuck Waldo," Finn hollered, "and fuck me!"

They were laughing as they raced down the hallway.

"Which room shall we christen?" Bran asked.

Rick gave them both a coy look and opened the basement door. "Great pleasures are to be found below if you dare." Rick began to descend the stairs.

Bran looked at Finn.

"After you," Finn bobbed his head.

Bran was excited, his cock was hard, and he found it a little difficult to keep his breathing steady. Not only was he going to get the chance to fuck Rick, he was going to, after all this time, have Finn as well.

When Bran got to the basement, he glanced around him with some pride. The 'dungeon' as they called it was really something to behold. With the help of Rick's consultant friend, the place was enough to turn on both sadist and masochist alike.

Against the wall were shackles and chains, and if that wasn't enough, there were wrist constraints dangling from the ceiling in the middle of the room and some sort of bar to keep your legs apart. There were all kinds of toys, masks, ball gags, butt plugs, and whips. There was even a rubber suit. On the other side was a padded table where one could really have some fun . . . stirrups, and cock rings abounded.

Rick was taking off his clothes. He smiled at Bran. "Come on, stop teasing me." He stood there naked now, and Finn walked right over and manhandled Rick's cock.

Okay. That was fast.

Bran stripped off and began to undress Finn. Finn looked at him and then kissed Bran hard. After the heated kiss, Bran looked at Rick. "I have some ideas. I would like to see you on that table over there."

Rick winked at him.

Finn pulled Bran up against him and kissed him again. He ran his hands over him as they moved across the room.

Rick jumped up on the table.

He had a great body, nicely toned, and his erection was really inviting. "Lie down," Bran told him.

Finn went to the other side of the table.

Rick lay on his back.

"Legs up," Finn said to Rick.

He lifted his legs into the sling and Bran pulled the rope to pull him higher so that his ass was also accessible.

"Look," Finn said, "you can lower the bottom."

The bottom end fell away, and Bran moved right up between Rick's thighs. "My cock is at a real good place right now," he said.

Finn was kissing Rick. Bran watched him move his hands over Rick's chest and play roughly with his nipples. Finn looked at Bran. "Want to clamp them. We have those, don't we Rick?"

Rick smiled. "Yeah. Over there on that shelf."

Finn went to get those, and Bran ran his hands up the inside of Rick's thighs, then let his fingers tickle along his shaft, then around the helmet-shaped head of his cock. Then he squeezed Rick's balls.

Rick met his gaze and licked his lips. "Um, that was nice."

"Lube, Finn," Bran called out. He could hardly breathe anymore. "I'm going to make him moan."

Rick smiled.

Finn brought lube.

Bran squeezed some on his finger and went up inside of Rick. Rick let out some breath. Finn began to rub and pinch Rick's nipples, then leaned in to lick each one. Bran pushed two fingers up into Rick.

Rick cried out softly now.

"Are you a slut?" Bran whispered. "Meow for me, baby."

Rick purred.

Finn rubbed and pulled some more on Rick's nipples. "Nice," Finn said. "Very nice." He pulled the left one out and clamped it.

Rick grunted. "Oh . . . yeah."

At the same time, Bran pushed two fingers up inside Rick and began to play with his cock, alternate stroking with some jerking.

Finn pulled out the other nipple and clamped it.

Bran began to aggressively fuck Rick's ass with his fingers. "Finn, bring me one of those sex toys, the largest one." He looked at Rick. "You liked being fucked?"

"Oh yeah." He nodded.

"Coat it with some of that lube," he told Finn. "I'll fuck this beautiful ass of his, and you go to his head. "You're going to suck Finn's cock, baby," Bran told him.

Rick licked his lips.

Bran waited until Finn lowered his cock over Rick's lips, then he pushed the slick vibrating monster up inside of him. It was the most erotic thing he'd ever seen. He almost came as he fucked Rick's ass with the dildo and Rick sucked Finn's cock with vigor. While he did, Rick moaned deep in his chest, his hips slamming up and down on the padded table.

Bran pulled out the dildo and guided his cock into Rick's ass. His eyes closed. Around him, the sounds of moaning and pleasure filled his ears. He was in another world. He came hard and fast.

Finn walked over and kissed him again. Rick was down. He hopped off the table and looked at Bran. "Okay, baby, your turn."

Bran blinked. "No, I . . ." But he had no time to protest. Finn and Rick put him on the table and pulled his wrists over his head. Before he knew it, his legs were in the stirrups, his ass, and cock on display. He was still reeling from the aftermath of orgasm, and Rick and Finn's hands moving over his body was sending shivers up and down his spine.

One of them was playing with his cock. He tried to see, but Finn placed a blindfold on his eyes.

"Hey," he protested. No one was listening.

His ass was being spread and thoroughly licked, then he felt a greased butt plug pushing up inside him. "Hey, guys." He wiggled.

"Gag him," Finn said.

A ball gag went inside his mouth.

"Get ready for the ride of your life," Rick said. The butt plug began to vibrate, and someone wrapped a strap around his cock.

"You'll come when we say, slut." That was Finn calling him a slut. But he felt dirty and horny and oh so sexy. This was hot. He'd never experienced anything like this before. Utter helplessness. *Touch me.*

Fingers were playing with his nipples, whispering the dirtiest things in his ear. "So hot, your nipples so hard and excited. Your cock is leaking. You want it. You want it bad."

Someone straddled his neck. The ball gag came out, and a cock lowered into his mouth. He sucked with pleasure as someone handled his cock and his balls then played with the plug in his ass.

One cock came out of his mouth, and another went in. At the same time, the plug was pulled out of his ass and the strap taken off his cock. He was being fucked. He didn't know who was inside of him, but they were fucking him hard and deep, stretching him wide. They knew how to fuck.

The cock came out of his mouth, and he cried out with orgasm. He lay there trying to get his breath back, and the mask came off. Finn kissed him. "Are you happy?"

Bran nodded. "Oh yeah."

"Good," Finn said. "My turn. And don't hold back."

CHAPTER THREE

Bran could hardly believe how many people had sexual fetishes they needed to indulge in secret. Even on the opening night, their new patrons seemed to have found a refuge in The Fetish Café, so much so, that Bran, Finn, and Rick wondered what their clients did before they came here.

Finn seemed to excel in dealing with clients who wanted to be slaves. Bran watched in some surprise as Finn roughly manhandled two brothers who wanted to be dressed in latex and chained up in a dungeon.

It was quite funny to see these same men chowing down on lush desserts and coffee by the pool after their session. They gave Finn a very nice tip. He was not a cruel Dom. In fact, he was more the head-master-punishing-the school-boy type.

"If you don't eat all your profiteroles," Bran overheard Finn telling the men, "You'll get a spanking."

Rick, too, quickly adapted to his new role. He seemed to attract foot fetish people, though in real life he professed to not understand the mania for expensive shoes. "I'd rather take you to dinner somewhere nice than buy a pair of Blahniks," he told Bran between clients.

Finn rolled his eyes when he heard Rick say this. Bran practically swooned.

He was already crazy about Rick and was amazed to find his own niche: food fetishes.

Bran was surprised how many people ate in secret, but then when he thought about it, this made sense since nobody in LA ate in public. In a town obsessed with thinness, people would meet for meals that mostly remained unconsumed. They'd order a plate of French fries to share, then pick at them, gazing longingly at the remaining portion. Now that he thought about it, he should have guessed sooner why so many food truck businesses and roadside hotdog and taco stands did so well in this city. People would shell out a fortune for meals they didn't eat in front of one another, then drive off to Pink's Hotdogs or Henry's Tacos and load up on fast food in virtual anonymity.

But not here.

Here at The Fetish Café, they could order decadent sweets, more than once, if they chose, and nobody batted an eye. Bran, Finn, and Rick could barely keep up with the orders, or the steady stream of newcomers. Finn had to make a pastry shop run a couple of times and had to resort to Ralph's grocery store at midnight to purchase cookies and donuts. No matter. Their clients ate everything.

With whipped cream.

And gusto.

Bran hadn't really given much thought to the idea that in his new job he'd be providing sex to his customers. He felt a bit odd about that since he was really a one-man kind of guy, but he discovered the food fetishists liked their food with sex served on the side. He got away with feeding them cake from his fingers, kissing them, and throwing in a hand-job. They were ecstatic. He gave several of those and two blow jobs. Sometimes he didn't have to do either. Mostly, they just wanted fun with food. By the end of the night, he'd made an appointment with a very nice Japanese businessman for the following evening.

They'd just swapped succulent kisses and bites of Napoleons, but the man had something else in mind.

"Have you ever tried *nantaimori*?" Mr. Toshiri asked.

Damn. What the hell is that? I thought I'd memorized all the sexual fetishes. Bran stared at his client as he hunted through his well-educated memory bank. "Do you perhaps mean *nyotaimori?*"

The man smiled. "That is the female version. *Nantaimori* is the male version."

Bran nodded. "I would be happy to assist you with that." He'd just agreed to be his client's human sushi platter.

When Mr. Toshiri paid, he gave Bran another kiss and said, "And please call me Kenji." He kissed Bran's hand. "I look forward to tomorrow night."

"As do I," Bran said, staggered at the two-hundred dollar tip that far exceeded the food Kenjo had consumed. He began to plot the *nantaimori* he would provide. He knew these were all the rage in some Asian restaurants in Tokyo, and probably here in California for all he knew. He agreed because he knew Kenji would pay, but also, because he wanted to give the man what he wanted. That got him thinking. He, Finn, and Rick would need to add to the menu. No problem. He'd take care of it in the morning.

They closed the club at three a.m. so the neighbors wouldn't squawk. This was, after all, a residential neighborhood. The three amigos sat in the kitchen and calculated their earnings. More than any of them had imagined.

Rick brewed tea for them as they discussed the evening's events. The biggest problem had been parking. They didn't want to hire a professional valet service and draw attention to the business.

"I know a guy," Rick said. "He has a business that provides discreet parking for private events. That will free up our staff."

"Exactly," Bran responded. "We didn't know what to expect."

They all agreed a secret Facebook group and an app would be essential to keep their clients informed of different, upcoming events.

"We want them to feel they're part of a secret fetish club. We want them to feel special," Finn said.

"And we're gonna need a couple of extra hands in the kitchen," Rick added. "For now."

They would definitely need help with the food. They'd crashed into each other in the kitchen all night lifting pastries out of bakery boxes. They'd need to hire extra help. The staff they'd brought in all ended up waiting on customers, as well as greeting guests and handling parking chores. Rick and Finn agreed that Bran could upgrade the menu to include savory appetizers.

"Who knows?" Rick said as he poured green tea for each of them. "We can put *nantaimori* on the menu. See if others like it. Maybe we can make a sweet version of it with chocolate-covered fruit and petit fours, or something."

"That's a wonderful idea," Bran said, sitting up straighter now. We almost ran out of food tonight. I've been Googling food fetishism. There are people that will pay to lick stuff like custard or chocolate pudding off your body."

"I can't believe we've successfully found a niche market so soon." Finn sipped at his tea. "I mean, most restaurants flounder in their first six months here. If they last a year they're lucky. The way we're going, I can't see a reason it won't work."

Rick shrugged. "Sex sells."

"Right. And we *are* selling sex." Bran grinned at Rick. He wouldn't mind a bit of sex with this hot guy right now, but he was exhausted.

"You two up for some fun?" Finn asked, glancing from Bran to Rick.

Rick shot Bran an appraising look, apparently realizing that Bran wasn't excited by the idea and said, "Raincheck. Right now, I feel like I got hit by a steam roller."

He and Bran pocketed their tips, and Finn shut down the computer.

"You guys are welcome to stay the night. There's plenty of room." Finn gestured to the sofa. "Bran always crashes here, but there are guest bedrooms upstairs, and we do need to get an early start tomorrow. We need to clean up the house, upgrade the menu and print it out, and of course, shop for food."

Bran's mind swirled with ideas and little worries. They wouldn't make money if they kept running out to buy store-bought cakes all night. Maybe they should hire a pastry chef.

"This sofa looks real good right now." He reached over to pat the soft cushions.

"Don't be silly." Rick grabbed his hand. "Let's bunk upstairs."

If Finn was upset about being rebuffed and his friends paring off, he didn't show it. In fact, he was already preparing a list of things they'd need. "Nine o'clock," he warned. "I expect you both down here first thing to help me delegate the day's tasks."

"No problem," Bran said.

"We'll be here." Rick gave him a wave. "Slave driver," he whispered under his breath as he led Bran up the stairs. Bran laughed until Rick silenced him with a kiss.

They put clean sheets on one of the guest beds and stripped off quickly. They began to kiss and fell into the bed, but neither had the energy even for a quickie.

"Turn over," Rick said, "I want to spoon you."

"Okay." Bran yawned. He complied, falling asleep with Rick's arms wrapped tightly around him.

Bran awoke, swearing he'd just closed his eyes, except that sunlight was streaming into the room. He could no longer feel Rick beside him. He turned to look. Nope. Gone.

He heard voices downstairs, dressed quickly and took the stairs two at a time.

"One of the neighbors left a note on the windshield of my car," Finn said as Bran strolled into the kitchen.

"Complaining about the noise?" Bran asked, reaching for the just-brewed pot of coffee.

"No. He wants to come to the party tonight." Finn gave him a sunny smile. "He's friends with your client. Mr. Toshiri."

"That's good." Bran poured himself some coffee, aware of Rick's gaze, but unable to read it.

"I've been doing some research, and we can buy a lot of our products from Restaurant Depot," Finn said. "They're like Home Depot, except they service the food industry. We're going to make sure we don't run out of food. I think we'll also need a wholesale candle dealer and we'll need to make a run to the flower market downtown a couple of times a week."

"Sounds good." Bran sipped his coffee.

"I contacted my friend Greg, and his crew will start valet service tonight. They will keep things quiet and make sure nobody gets upset." He paused. "I'm so glad we don't serve booze. Drunk drivers are a problem we won't have."

"And what have you achieved this morning?" Finn asked Bran.

Bran raised a brow at his friend. "Two sips of coffee. That's pretty good, considering I just woke up."

Finn tried so hard to look stern but just laughed.

After Rick and Bran had returned to their respective homes and had showered and changed, the three men met at the Restaurant Depot to purchase all the food they'd need for the next few days. Bran was pleased to see huge platters of sushi at decent prices. They loaded up on pastries and res-taurant-sized containers of refrigerator biscuits to make flattened ham and cheese sandwiches. They bought gigantic bars of chocolate, instant custard powder, cream, ice cream, coffee, and tea. They discussed purchasing a cappuccino machine at some point and decided they'd rent one and see if it garnered extra sales.

They spent all day cleaning and preparing the house for the festivities that night.

Bran was grossed out by all the spent condoms he found scattered by the pool cabanas and in all the wastebaskets throughout the main house.

"At least they're practicing safe sex," Finn said. "Maybe we should hire a maid.

"I know a woman who'll help us," Rick told them. "We can't go through this every single day. Maybe we can ask Ana to come in the mornings for three or four hours."

"That will eat into our income, but I agree, we need help," Finn said. "I think we're going to need a second fridge and a freezer. What do you guys think?"

"A second dishwasher might be useful, too," Bran suggested.

"We've got two kitchen staff hired for tonight. We'll see how they feel at the end of the shift," Rick said. His tone was a bit snappish, which surprised Bran. What was up with Rick, anyway?

He didn't have much time to reflect on it, because their cell phones began ringing with new people wanting to come tonight. Bran was surprised to receive a call from pop singer Brenda Bright, whom he'd met at Paul's store. He felt a stab of grief for his former boss, unable to shake the pain of witnessing the man's gruesome murder.

"Jack and I want to come to your new club," she said. "Are you still making women's shoes for men?"

Bran didn't know what to say. He was no cobbler, and although he had Paul's client list, he hadn't contacted any of them. He wondered how Brenda had gotten his private number, then remembered they'd spoken on the phone when he'd helped ship thigh-high boots to Jack Tappin in Honolulu.

"Well, we might," Bran said, wondering if he could actually find somebody to carry on Paul's work. He had a lot of shoes in his apartment. He'd tossed them into Paul's car the night he'd left the store. He hadn't been back since.

"So, can we come tonight?" she asked. "Jack is desperate to have some fun with Rick."

How did she know Rick's real name? How did she know him at all?

"Keni Toshiri is a very good friend of mine," Brenda said, apparently reading his thoughts. "He had a wonderful time and said you are very discreet."

Bran didn't think he could say no to the pop singer, and couldn't fight the small feeling of jealousy when Rick acted enthusiastic about fooling around with the sexy Jack Tappin.

"She's cool. She's welcome here," Rick said. "Of course, she'll have to pay for it."

Bran left Finn and Rick to deal with the particulars as he prepared himself for the live sushi platter he'd have to be in just a few hours. He bathed very carefully with a fragrance-free soap, making sure he didn't slather on a scented deodorant that would emit a perfumed smell or taste bad and interfere with Kenji's enjoyment of his unusual meal.

At Finn's suggestion, he wore no deodorant at all. "Once you're done you can shower and change," Finn said.

At a quarter to nine, guests started arriving and the kitchen staff, two wonderful young men, named Augie and Lewis, showed up, brandishing teeny maid outfits, high heels, and huge smiles. Bran warmed to the guys immediately. They helped Bran set up in one of the cabana rooms. They placed him naked on a massage table and sprayed him with ice cold water before beginning the process of covering his body with pieces of sushi and sashimi.

"The room is freezing." Bran shivered involuntarily.

"We have to keep it cold until your guest arrives," Augie said. "The most important thing is you can't move. You have to stay still."

"Did you have to say that? Now I'm beset by the urge to run around the room," Bran complained.

He closed his eyes, nervous as hell. Ever since Brenda's call, he kept seeing flashes of Paul in his mind. He wished so strongly that his boss were still alive. Paul had been good and kind.

If I end up being half the boss he was, my staff will be very lucky indeed.

He glanced down and realized the men were placing the sushi on strategic places, pulse points on his body.

"The best pieces of tuna go on your crotch," Augie said, with a grin. A few minutes later he added, "All done," his tone cheerful. "You're making me hungry just looking at you." He brushed a strand of hair out of Bran's eyes. "Why are you shaking so badly?"

"I told you, I'm cold."

"A little bit nervous, too?" Augie kept stroking Bran's forehead with soothing fingers.

Bran nodded.

"Relax. You'll find that it's quite a turn on being a sushi platter. And as for staying warm, keep your hands by your sides–"

"I am."

"Right. But also do this." Augie held up his right hand. "Tuck your thumb into your fist. It helps regulate your body temperature."

"Okay, thanks."

"I have to run. Finn's about to be covered in warm chocolate in the cabana next door. A new clients wants to put whipped cream and ice cream all over him and lick it from his body."

Bran nodded, tucking his thumbs into his fists, as advised. He found it worked, and as he grew a little warmer, began to relax. He was afraid to close his eyes in case he saw poor Paul's face, but sleepiness overcame him. A few seconds later a voice said in his ear,

"Good evening."

Bran almost leaped off the table in shock. He recognized Kenji's voice immediately and returned the greeting.

Kenji stood over him, giving Bran a light kiss. "Very, very nice. Somebody knows the correct placement for the yellow-tail sashimi." He reached for a pair of chopsticks on the serving table beside Bran and lifted a piece to his lips. Bran watched his client inhale the slice.

"Your body heat makes it the perfect temperature," Kenji informed him. He fed Bran a piece. Bran dutifully chewed and swallowed. He had to admit the raw fish tasted buttery and fresh and went down effortlessly.

Kenji bent to lick up a piece of salmon directly from Bran's left nipple.

Bran reacted to the unexpected touch of the man's tongue on his body. Kenji licked at various pieces of sushi, savoring each bite. He slowly, maddeningly, took his time reaching Bran's crotch, where he licked at a row of tiny pieces of tuna sashimi.

"Hmmm . . . delicious."

Bran gasped as Kenji delved lower, his lips and tongue nibbling at other pieces of sushi, then, Bran's cock. He almost jumped from the table, aware that his cock had sprung into action. Kenji sure seemed to appreciate it. He licked and kissed Bran's hard shaft, his eyes closing in apparent pleasure as he began sucking him.

As quickly as he started, he released Bran, then moved

down his body, licking something from Bran's balls.

Kenji murmured his delight as he scraped his tongue across Bran's balls and back again. He returned to Bran's cock, covering the bobbing head with his mouth. He began to suck Bran with tentative reverence, then, increasing pressure, moving up and down, his mouth a tight, warm, O.

Bran fought from coming but couldn't. The sensation of Kenji's probing fingertips stroking between his legs and deep between his ass cheeks drove him over the edge.

Kenji began working on Bran's hole, moaning as he kept sucking and stroking.

Bran came violently in the man's mouth as Kenji slid two fingers into him. Kenji did not release him until he'd coaxed a second orgasm from him, then took his mouth off Bran's cock to finish eating the remaining two pieces of dragon roll sushi nestled in the crooks of Bran's inner elbows. He almost came again.

"Perfect," Kenji whispered into Bran's ear, kissing it. "I'd like to book again for tomorrow night, please." And with that, he slipped out of the door.

Bran showered and dressed, feeling shaky from the encounter. His cock was still hard. How was this possible?

He could hear moans coming from next door. As he finished buttoning his Levi's, he walked outside and found Rick dressed in a maid's outfit, sitting at a poolside table feeding pastries to a client. A closer glance in the dark and Bran realized the client was Jack Tappin, dressed in a thigh-high skirt and lace-up boots. Bran averted his gaze and gave Rick a smile, but didn't get one back.

What the fuck ever.

He walked into the house and saw that the place was hopping. People streamed in and out of the doors. A hand gripped his arm. He turned, happy to see Brenda.

"Doesn't my man look happy?" she asked.

"Yes, he does."

She pouted a little. "I'm sorry about Paul. I really liked him. Say, do you have any of his shoes?"

"I grabbed a few. Why?"

"There's one custom order I never got. Baby blue suede ankle boots."

"I can check in the morning."

"They're not here?"

He shook his head. For some reason, he didn't feel comfortable telling her where they were. He saw a client from last night beckoning him. "Is there anything I can get you right now? Coffee, dessert?"

"Oh, no. I'm having a lot of fun indulging my voyeurism."

"I'll be in touch," he told Brenda, kissing her on the cheek. He walked over to his beckoning client. "Good evening," he told the man, accepting his kiss on the cheek. "How are you?"

"Better now you're here. Any chance of a piece of cheesecake?"

"Would you like coffee with that?"

"Please." The man beamed at him.

In the kitchen, Augie and Lewis were frantically loading up dishes. Augie looked mutinous when Bran asked about cheesecake.

"One slice left," he said. "I've never gone through so much food in my life." He handed Bran the last remaining piece of Cheesecake Factory chocolate chip cookie dough cheesecake and banished Bran from the kitchen.

Back in the living room, he placed the cake plate on the table, moving to the sideboard to pour coffee for his client.

"Sit on my lap," the man said. Bran obeyed his wishes. From his perch, he could look straight out into the backyard and watched Jack Tappin practically devour Rick's mouth with his.

I wonder what Brenda thinks about that. He glanced around and saw that the songstress had one of their two waitresses pressed against the wall. They rubbed up against one another, kissing each other frantically.

On the staircase, Finn was making out with a guy.

Holy cow. It's Waldo. What the hell's he doing here? I hope he's paying for that kiss.

Bran soon had to focus on his client, a shy man he recalled was some kind of romance writer.

"I had dreams of you last night," the man said. Bran couldn't for the life of him recall the guy's name. Mark? Mike? Mack? It was one of the three.

"Could you ever consider dancing with me?" the guy asked.

"Dancing with you? Sure."

"I mean lap dancing. I want to fuck you with you on my lap."

Bran blinked. He would prefer to feed the guy cake. Let him eat it. Let them all eat it. He picked up the plate and flicked his fingertip across the cookie crumbed-top of the cake.

"Here baby, suck this."

The man complied. He got so turned on sucking Bran's fingers that his cock hardened in his pants. Bran could feel it. He writhed back and forth to the tune of some Justin Bieber song on the sound system. The man clutched his hips and rubbed himself harder against Bran. He came quickly, saying over and over, "That's so good. Oh yes. That's so good."

Bran didn't mind. He preferred getting the guy's rocks off this way rather than the traditional way.

"I have a confession," the client said. "I'm usually into feederism, but you really rocked my world." He picked up the menu. "What other types of dessert do you have?"

He picked a Napoleon and Bran went off to the kitchen.

He paused just inside to Google feederism. My God. It was people who received sexual gratification from fucking fat people.

Does this mean we'll have to get a couple of them on staff? He pondered this as he rifled through a pastry box.

"Hey," a voice said.

Bran looked up to see Rick watching him from the doorway.

"Hey yourself," Bran said, discarding the empty box. Once again, they seemed to have run out of food.

"How did it go?" Rick asked.

"The sushi platter?" Bran grinned. "It was pretty good fun, actually."

Rick scowled. "Did you make it with him?"

"What?" Bran stared at him as the kitchen staff ran rings around them.

"You heard. Did he fuck you?"

"Nope." Bran scoured through other boxes for any tasty treat he could feet his client. "Sucked me off though." He resisted saying, "Twice."

"You enjoy it?"

"What?" Bran asked again. What was going on with this guy?

"If you two are gonna have a lovers quarrel do it somewhere else, please." Augue pointed the way out of the kitchen.

"No quarrel," Bran said. "Do we have any Napoleons left?"

"This is your lucky day. We have three left." Augie served one up on a glass dish.

Bran took it, allowing Rick to steer him into the hallway.

"What's going on?" Bran asked as Rick pushed him to the wall and began to kiss him. Bran almost dropped the plate.

Their ragged kiss went on, before they broke off, both

breathing heavily.

"That's what's going on. I can't stop thinking about you," Rick said. "I fucking can't stand the idea of some other guy being near you."

"Yeah. And it really looked that way when you were giving Jack Tappin a tonsillectomy."

Rick bent his forehead to Bran's. "I didn't fuck him."

"Good."

Rick stared into Bran's eyes. They had a big problem on their hands. They were only on their second night and were already experiencing stupid, passion-killing feelings of jealousy.

Bran shook his head. He couldn't walk away from this lucrative business because he liked a guy. Nah-ah. He'd struggled too long. He thought of Paul's extinguished dreams and realized he had to live life for both of them.

"I can't do this right now," he said. "I have a client waiting."

"Fine. I have clients, too. And I won't say no when they want to fuck me."

"That's fine. Really fine." Bran hated lying, but he had to get used to the idea that this was why they were all here. He pushed Rick off him, ignoring the man's soft pleas.

"Bran, talk to me. Come back."

He shook his head. He couldn't stop now. He had to work. He pasted a smile on his face and returned to his client, who was licking his lips.

"That looks good. I was beginning to worry that maybe you wouldn't come back. I know how popular you are." He looked so anxious that Bran laughed, nestling back in his lap. He kissed his client but still couldn't remember his name.

"I'll always be here for you," he said. "I'll always come back." He began rubbing his ass back and forth against the man's crotch. He caught the spark of desire igniting in the man's eyes.

The client swallowed hard. "God, you're sexy. I've never wanted anyone so much."

Bran smiled and kissed the guy hard. He tried not to think of Rick and sleeping in his arms. He caught a glimpse of Rick across the room, watching him. The music changed to some club song he didn't recognize.

Waldo and Finn had vanished from the stairs. Bran saw a scowling Waldo standing against the wall, arms folded.

Uh-oh. Another unhappy customer. Bran heard Finn's mad laugh and glanced over to where Finn was feeding cake to the two brothers from the previous night. They licked at his fingers in an intimate way.

Bran glanced from one table to the next, heard the laughter and impassioned cries from various points around the house.

His client began to nuzzle his throat.

"Feed me," the man begged.

Bran broke off a piece of pastry all gooey with icing. He held it to his client's lips, and his heart gave a lurch when he noticed Jack Tappin had caught up with Rick and the two men were dancing arm in arm, even though the music was fast-paced. Jack squeezed Rick's ass cheek. As they moved around, Bran could see that Rick had both of his hands on Jack's ass cheeks.

Bran swallowed over the lump in his throat. He gazed at the feverish sexual activity around them and wondered, for one fearful moment, could this business really last? Could they do it? Could he, Finn, and Rick run this place without their feelings becoming trampled?

Chapter Four

This was a nightmare, a moment when Bran knew some things seemed to be coming together and yet everything else could be falling apart. Bran slumped on the sofa, relishing the sublime silence. Everyone had gone now, including the staff. Finn was somewhere in the kitchen and Rick had left when the work was done, without so much as a word.

A terrible headache threatened, and Bran had drunk down what was left of a half-filled bottle of champagne. That took the edge off but was about to cause him to have a head-on collision with pain. "I can't fucking win for losing!"

"What?" Finn poked his head in the living room. "Did you say something?"

"Yeah, and never mind." Bran rubbed his temples.

Finn heaved a heavy sigh. He took the chair facing Bran, and they sat there in absolute silence for the longest time. Then Finn broke it with a bang. "You're in love with Rick."

Bran paused and glanced at him. "Says who?"

"The look on your face."

"Yeah, and what about Waldo?" There was an accusing tone in his voice.

"I'm going to ignore that."

"I figured you would."

"At one time I thought you wanted me."

Bran glared at him. "If you thought that, why didn't you do something about it?"

"I was afraid it would ruin our friendship."

Bran considered that then nodded.

"Listen." Finn leaned forward resting his elbows on his knees. He looked tired. "This is going to turn out to be a virtual goldmine. Love is going to mess it all up. You know that, don't you?"

"Fuck." Bran sighed. "I never wanted to be a participant. I just wanted to be a manager. How in the hell did I end up being someone's appetizer?"

Finn laughed. "It was fun though."

"Yeah." Bran smiled.

"The question is, are you going to throw this all away because of Rick? I think we should . . . end our arrangement with him."

"We can't do that." Bran shook his head. "We initially cut him in. He helped make all this happen. We couldn't have done it without him. How can we push him out?"

"Okay, you're right. We could make him work from outside, increasing our clientele, doing payroll and such."

"But he's a main attraction."

"We'll find others."

"And what about Waldo? How did he end up here anyway? I thought it was over."

"So did I," Finn said. "He told me he made a mistake. He wants to start over."

"Oh. What did you tell him?"

"I'm game, but . . . he doesn't want me doing this. So, if he makes me choose, I choose this. Question is"—he stood—"do you?"

Money or love. What a choice. Didn't one need both?

Finn was staring at him. Bran met his gaze. "We have to choose this, or else we live hand to mouth again, and I don't want that."

"I don't either. So we're agreed. This is top priority."

Yes, but what did they do about their hearts?

Bran nodded and got to his feet. He'd sleep here tonight. He was too tired to go home. "You mind?" He glanced at the ceiling.

Finn understood the message. He held out his hand. Bran took it, and they climbed the stairs. The sun was coming up.

In the bedroom, they stripped off their clothes and cuddled close together under the blankets. Bran looked at Finn. "You still love him then?"

Finn nodded silently.

Bran made a sound that could have been a laugh but ended up being a sob. "Aren't we a pair?"

Finn pressed his forehead against Bran's and nodded. "Sleep now. We have much to do tomorrow, my friend."

Bran's eyes closed. He saw Rick. He swore at the image in his head. Why'd he have to fuck everything up for? Damn it. How long could they last working together every night watching each other be someone else's sexual cookie? Eventually, exhaustion overcame him, and coherent thought deserted him, but his unconscious mind was restless.

When he awoke, Bran struggled to a sitting position to see Finn standing in the room drying off from a shower. "Ah, what time is it?"

"Seven o'clock. Another shift starting soon. Man, sleeping with you is like sleeping with a wrestler. You tossed and turned and mumbled in your sleep half the day. I eventually went to sleep down the hall."

"Sorry." Bran rubbed his eyes.

"What's on the agenda?"

"Well, we have enough food, but the place needs to be cleaned again. I picked up some last night but was too tired to do it all. You think Rick will bring that Ana woman today?"

"I don't know. I'm going to look into hiring a good pastry chef. We have a state-of-the-art kitchen. We shouldn't have to run out every day to the bakery."

"Great. Where do we go for that?"

"I'll check online at those places where people upload their resumes, and there is also the Cordon Bleu Institutes. I could call and find a moonlighter."

"Great idea. Take a shower and get dressed, I'll make us some breakfast."

Bran slipped out of bed. He took a long time in the shower, the warm spray dragging his brain out of the fog. When he slid the door open, he was surprised to have someone hand him a towel.

"Rick?" He took the towel from him.

Rick leaned back against the vanity, arms akimbo. "Finn said you wanted to talk to me."

Bran clumsily wrapped the towel around his waist. Rick looked good enough to eat, pardon the pun, with his faded blue jeans and white muscle shirt. His hair was a little wind-blown, and he hadn't shaved.

Bran hoped the hell he could hide his erection. He opened the medicine cabinet, angry at himself for his lack of discipline. And damn that Finn. He didn't mean for Rick to come into the bathroom when he was half-dressed to have a discussion.

Rick pushed a can a shaving cream at him.

Bran slammed the cabinet door. "I don't want that."

"You're angry."

Bran eyed the open door. "This could have waited."

"Okay." Rick pushed off the vanity and headed for the door.

Bran reached out and grabbed his arm.

Rick paused, glanced back at him. "What?"

"We have to talk."

"So talk." He pulled his arm away.

"I want this."

Rick met his gaze. "You want what, the business or me?"

"Why in hell do I have to choose?"

"Then don't." He shrugged.

"I think you should . . . well, Finn and I were talking and—"

"He told me. You want me to work outside. That's fine." He looked away. "So the discussion is over."

"No, it's not over." Bran shook his head. "There has to be a way for us to have it all."

"What if there's not?" Rick looked at him again. "You've already made your choice, haven't you?"

"I . . . well . . . I . . . it's not a choice and . . . I . . ."

"Save it," he said. "Listen, I brought Ana, she'll do the cleaning up in the morning. I trust her. She used to work for my granny. You can give her a key, and she'll come in early and have everything cleaned before you guys get up."

"You guys?"

"I know you slept here last night. In fact, Finn is a logical choice for you."

"It's not like that."

"You don't have to justify anything to me. Anyway, back to Ana, give her a key, she'll do a good job, and she's discreet."

"Okay. We'll pay her well."

Bran watched Rick leave the bathroom. He swore under his breath and chased after him. "Rick," he said just as Rick got to the bedroom door. "The customers love you. What do we do about that?"

He didn't turn around. "We could schedule alternate times so that we don't run into each other."

Bran's heart was breaking.

"Listen, you don't want to see me, and believe me"—he paused—"I don't want to see you fulfilling every guy's deepest kink, so . . . schedule things and let me know. I'm going. I'm going to try to puff up our client list. Good luck tonight."

He was gone. Bran sank down on the side of the bed and put his face in his hands. This hurt, but he told himself it would get better and it would become just business between them again.

He took a moment to recover and went down into kitchen. He half hoped Rick would still be around, but he was gone. Finn was sharing a cup of coffee with a soft-spoken, middle-aged women with mauve streaks in her dark hair.

"Bran, this is Ana."

Bran shook her hand. She held onto his for a while and stared into his eyes. "It will be all right, Bran," she said.

Bran blinked. "I beg your pardon?"

Finn laughed. "Ana is an empath."

Ana didn't seem to appreciate the laugh, but Finn was a die-hard skeptic for anything that couldn't be scientifically explained.

"I just feel things," she contradicted Finn politely. "I read people's emotions and honey, you are on the down low."

Bran smiled politely. "I'm fine and thanks. We have a whole lot of clients coming through here in a few hours, so I think we should get working."

"Then I'd better get busy," she said. "Finn has been through the terms with me, and I've agreed. Look over what we've agreed, and if you're on board, we're good to go."

"Are you available in the evening as an extra dishwasher?" Bran asked, looking over points Finn had written down on paper. The salary was reasonable, and at an hourly rate. That was good because some days they'd need her more than others.

"I'll take all the work I can get." She smiled. "I'm helping my daughter put her son through cooking school."

"Cooking school?" Bran and Finn said at the same time.

She took a step back. "Yes." She smiled uncertainly.

"We're looking for a chef. Would he work here?" Bran

asked.

"If Carter can juggle it with his classes."

"Hours are flexible," Bran said. "He can make up the pastries beforehand and leave."

"I'll speak to him," Ana promised.

"This is great." Bran nodded. He put down the paper. "Welcome to the team."

She shook both their hands. "Now, show me your supplies, boys."

They laughed, and Finn escorted Ana to the utility cupboard where all the cleaning stuff was stored.

"Okay," Bran heard her announce, "outta my way, fellows, I'm good to go!"

He smiled and decided to check the special request box that they left for their clients. They could comment, make suggestions, all for the purpose of increasing client satisfaction. The first rule of business school was happy clients keep coming back.

Bran was deep into reading several of the comments, all of them positive when Finn came in with a three-layer praline cake. "Look at this baby!"

"Wow, where did you get that?"

"A special delivery from the bakery down the street, a thank you for our patronage, and a new client. The owner wants to come tonight."

"Splendid, that should satisfy the Sitophiles."

"People turned on by food," Finn said with a chuckle. "You've been studying up."

"Do you know what Sploshers are?"

"They love being wet and messy, mostly covered in food, but it can be mud or oil, even paint." Finn made a face. "Let's stick to food."

"I'm with you." Bran took the cake from Finn and sat it on the kitchen counter.

Finn took Bran's breakfast out of the oven, raisin French toast, smothered in butter and syrup. "Almost forgot."

"Um," Bran stuck his finger in the syrup and tasted it. "The real stuff."

"Of course."

They had more coffee, and Bran finished his French toast. He passed Finn the comment sheets. "We're on the right track. Some want more variety of strippers. They want to fondle and eat. Only men, but what if we get requests for women?"

"We'll get women." Finn grinned.

"Let me call Rick and see if we can hire a few strippers tonight. We'll chain a couple in the dungeon."

"Fun, okay, get on that," Finn said.

"I love Ana by the way," Bran called after him.

Finn was out of the room, but he hollered back. "Me, too!"

Bran picked up his cell phone and stared at Rick's number for a moment, then he pressed the speed dial. The phone rang a few times then went to voice mail. *You've reached Rick. You know the routine. Have a good one.*

"Damn it, Rick, are you avoiding me now?" Bran blinked. Why was he so angry? He hung up and stared at the phone as if that would make it ring. It didn't. "Don't call back," he said. He shoved it in his pocket. "I can get strippers if I want."

The phone rang. Bran pulled it back out of his pocket and stared at it. *Rick.* "There you are," Bran said.

He laughed.

"What are you laughing about?"

"What was the tantrum for?"

"Not a tantrum. I . . . well . . . I need you."

"I need you, too."

There was silence.

Bran cleared his throat. "I need you to get some male strippers. Clients want more accessories."

"How many you want?"

"Ah . . . two for the dungeon and maybe two up top, vary the look."

"Gotcha."

"Don't hang up."

"Okay."

"Say something."

"Hello, Bran."

Bran smiled. Damn it. He was in love.

"Can I go now?"

"No."

"Okay, but I'm on the freeway."

"Okay, I'll hang up. Rick, I don't want it to be this way."

"I hear you."

"I want my praline cake, and I want to eat you, too." Bran grinned then laughed when Rick said, "Eh?"

"Never mind. Hurry with the strippers, okay?"

"You in a hurry to see strippers, or to see me?"

"You."

"In that case, I'll be there very fast."

Bran blew an audible kiss in the phone.

Rick chuckled and hung up.

Bran was still cradling the phone when Finn walked back in. "You alright?"

"I love Rick," he announced. "I don't know how to do this, but I can't pretend I don't. And you love Waldo."

"Damn it, Bran, I thought we'd settled this." Finn looked discouraged. "Waldo won't take me back while I'm running this place. He's too . . . ah . . . uptight."

"Well, I'll figure out a way to make this work for both of us." Bran gave Finn a hopeful look. He didn't return it.

"Do what you want, Bran. But I know Waldo. Rick is hip, and as long as you guys can separate love and sex, you'd do okay maybe."

Bran shook his head. "I don't want Rick fucking other men. I almost lost it over the kissing last night, and I think it's the same for him."

"Clones? robots?" Finn attempted a joke. It fell flat.

"Maybe we can hire the sex workers and just manage."

"Okay, but clients request us. You need to put on an ugly suit," Finn told him.

"You too." Bran grinned.

Finn sobered.

"Rick's bringing strippers, maybe they'd serve the clients," Bran suggested.

"That's going to make a noticeable dent in our profits, Bran. We'll need to increase our clients tenfold if we're going to get rich off of this."

"Then there has to be a way to do just that."

"It will take time," Finn said. "Our expenses will be far more than what we take in."

"Look, I still have some money left, and I have . . . shit . . ." Bran clicked his fingers. "I have shoes worth a fortune. I say we sell them and I'll use the rest of my money. We'll take a loss for a while but we'll hiring good sex workers, regulars the clients will come to love. The three of us can work on increasing our client base, and within a month, we should be in the black again."

When Finn didn't comment, Bran asked, "Waldo will take you back if you are just a manager, won't he?"

Finn nodded. "He doesn't want me to . . . you know . . ."

"Okay then. It's perfect. Let's talk to Rick."

Two hours later, Rick arrived with four of the hottest male strippers Finn and Bran had ever seen. One African-American, one Asian, one White, and one Hispanic, all drop dead gorgeous.

"Okay," Rick said, "take 'em off boys and show my associates what you got."

Bran and Finn stood in awed silence. All were toned, buff, and had more than enough to fulfill any fantasy.

Finn pulled Rick over. "Will they do more than dance?"

"They'll do whatever you want." Rick winked.

Finn beamed.

Bran gave Finn a decided push forward. "Why don't you show them the ropes so to speak and I'll talk to Rick, tell him the latest."

Finn didn't need to be told twice.

Bran took Rick's arm and pulled him into the kitchen. He closed the door, threw his arms around his neck and kissed him passionately on the mouth.

When he let him up for air, Rick said, "I thought you wanted to talk."

"Fuck me first, talk later." Bran walked over to the counter where the beautiful praline cake was sitting. "Oh," he said, pretending to be disappointed, "look at that, this cake should have been put in the fridge, its gone soft." He pulled Rick to the counter and pushed his back up against it. He grabbed for his zipper and hauled it down, then yanked his pants and underwear to the floor. One look at Rick's cock was enough to send him to heaven. He reached behind him, grabbed a fistful of cake and smeared it all over Rick's cock and balls.

Rick laughed, trying to brush some off with his hands but Bran grabbed Rick's wrists and lifted his arms up on the counter. "Stay still. Sit up on the counter and keep your legs open, lean back on your palms. It's lunchtime."

The praline was delicious, but Rick tasted far better. Within minutes, Bran had a mouth full of come-laced praline heaven, and Rick moaned in pleasure. Bran crawled up over him on the counter, making Rick laugh. "You're a nut."

"Yes," Bran said. "I'm nuts for you."

"Aww," Rick exclaimed and pulled Bran down for a kiss.

Bran was more than happy to lie between Rick's sticky thighs and kiss him, although he was dreading what his own jeans were going to look like when they separated.

Suddenly they heard someone clear their throat rather loudly. Bran and Rick separated and looked up.

"Oh," Rick said, "it's only Finn." He pulled Bran in for more kisses.

Bran was laughing, struggling to break away.

Finally, Rick released him and Bran got on the floor.

Finn's eyes widened.

Bran looked down at his pants. "Guess I have to change," he said as Rick scrambled to cover himself.

"Guess so." Finn glanced at the cake, then at Rick. "It's in your hair."

Rick lifted a hand to his hair and grinned. "You like the strippers?"

"They're perfect," Finn said as Rick slid over the counter and pulled on his clothes.

"So," Rick asked, "what's the news?"

"Oh, yeah," Bran said. "I have a plan. Finn is willing to go along so that he can get Waldo back. And, well . . . I think this may be a solution for me and you."

Rick smiled. "So, there is a me and you?"

Bran nodded. "I hope so."

"Tell me your great plan," Rick rubbed his nose against Bran's.

Bran quickly explained how they would take a loss, increase their client base but just tend to the management.

"We need to make that clear to the clients," Rick pointed out.

"Rick," Finn said, "do you think we could increase our client base enough to support us all well and yet pay staff?"

"Eventually, yes." Rick nodded. He smiled at Bran. "Good plan, honey."

"You two!" Finn rolled his eyes.

"Go call Waldo," Bran grumbled.

"I will, but first we need to get things organized. Guests will be here in two hours."

Bran reluctantly gave Rick a final kiss. "I would love to continue our exploration later."

He winked. "I'm game, but I need to ah . . . shower off. And you, young man" — he turned him toward the door and patted his butt — "need to change your pants."

"Oh yeah." Bran smiled. He was so happy, he didn't even notice anymore, but the clients would.

He followed Rick upstairs, and Rick steered him away from the bathroom when Bran attempted to go in with him. "No, no, no, you're not coming in the bathroom with me, we'll never get back downstairs."

"Okay," he grumbled, "but it's torture."

"If we're going to make this work, we need to stay focused," Rick told him.

"You will fuck me after closing?" He met his gaze.

"Baby," he growled, "I'm going to fuck you for hours."

Bran made a face and tried to get closer. "Oh yeah?"

"Stop it. Go away," Rick told him, taking a step back, then he disappeared into the bathroom.

Bran heard the lock slip over the door. "Oh come off it," he called out.

The shower went on. Bran went to change his clothes with a big smile on his face.

Brenda Bright was the first one to show up. She was without her rapper boyfriend. "He's coming later," she said. "I want to buy him a surprise."

"I've got just the thing," Bran told her. "Come with me."

Bran had brought the ten pair of shoes into the house from his apartment, plus the ones he'd left in the trunk of

Paul's car, the car he still had parked in Finn's garage. Last count, there were seventeen boxes. He knew Brenda had ordered some. He hoped to hell the ones she wanted were among the ones he'd grabbed.

Brenda hovered anxiously over the bed of one of the upstairs rooms as Bran opened one box after another, saying a little prayer when Brenda's order of baby blue ankle boots were among the forage.

"Oh and you have Kirkwood, and Webster," she exclaimed, examining each shoe carefully. "That pair over there is definitely Gucci and one Marrant. Those boots, if I was to guess without peeking, I'd say were McQueen, or perhaps Marrant because Isabel is fond of booties."

"It's actually Saint Laurent," Bran said proudly.

"Good." She gave Bran a high five. "You're becoming an expert."

Not that he'd wear any of them. He checked the sizes. "You wear a seven right?"

"Sometimes." She grinned.

"The Kirkwood and Webster are sevens."

"Um, is that so?" She checked the others. "Two will fit Jack and the other my mom. Give me a deal. I'll take them all off your hands."

Bran was frantically trying to remember what these babies went for. The ones sold to the general public could go from between seven hundred to two grand, but these were specially made with a little extra, real diamonds and rubies. He was going to go with one hundred thousand dollars a pair. "Six hundred thousand, they're yours."

Bran held his breath as Brenda rubbed her chin, appearing to give it some thought. If she said yes, they were on their way. They could hire all the staff they needed and concentrate on expanding their clientele.

"I have a condition," she said, meeting his gaze.

"Shoot." Bran was getting excited. *Please, please, please.*

"I was looking for the ultimate birthday present for Jack, and I know what it is."

I raised an eyebrow.

"He wants to be used in the dungeon. He would come in dressed as a woman with a pair of fabulous shoes. Two hot naked men would feed him then start to paw him, and drag him down to the dungeon."

"I thought Jack was straight?"

"Oh, he is . . . or says he is, but deep down he fantasizes about getting molested by two hot men while in drag. It would have to look forced, and I'd have to be chained up, too, helpless to help him. Jack would get sexually worked over while I looked helplessly on. Can you handle that?"

"No sweat." Bran grinned.

"Well, you're on. I'll bring Jack on Saturday night, and I'll have my accountant draw up a check."

Bran hugged her tightly and kissed her on the forehead.

She seemed surprised but pleased.

"Ah . . ." Bran put up a hand. "I'd prefer cash if you don't mind. Paul gave me these shoes and . . . ah . . ." He didn't want to go into detail.

She nodded. "You'll have the money by early next week."

"Perfect." Bran beamed.

"When the accountant drops off the cash, he'll take the shoes." She grinned, hugging her booties.

"Great."

Bran could hardly contain himself until she left. He ran into the kitchen only to see Ana talking with a young man who was turning dough in one those complicated mixers.

"Bran," Ana said, "my grandson, Carter. Finn said to try him out, and he came right over."

The young man shook hands with Bran. "I'm happy to have the opportunity. I won't let you down. Finn gave me a list of pastries, and you're going to be impressed."

Ana looked proud. "I'm going back to cleaning," she said and scurried out of the kitchen.

"Wonderful," Bran said. "Thank you."

Rick was getting the strippers orientated, so Bran didn't interrupt him. He found Finn in the office putting together bills. "I have to tell you something," Bran said, hanging on the door.

Finn looked up. "What?"

"I got the money to keep us going. I sold Paul's really expensive shoes to Brenda Bright. We're going to be okay to pay the staff for at least a few months."

Finn plunked down in the chair and let out a big puff of air. "Thank the heavens! How did you manage it?"

"Just did," Bran beamed. "Call Waldo okay?"

Finn smiled. "Okay."

"I promised that we'd do Jack up on Saturday night, some kind of forced sex thing. It's his birthday. Brenda wants to be chained, too . . . to watch."

"Whatever floats their boat." Finn laughed.

"It's a freebie."

"No problem."

"Okay, I got something I need to do. I'll be back soon."

"Everything is under control," Finn said, picking up the phone.

Bran wanted them to be happy, and he knew Finn loved Waldo. Bran certainly felt like he really had fallen hard for Rick. In the garage, Bran examined Paul's car. He couldn't keep it, and even though Paul's killers had been arrested, it would cause suspicion to have it here. He needed to get rid of it. Maybe he could sell it. No. Best thing was to remove the license plate and all traces of Paul and abandon it somewhere. That made him feel guilty. He already had had to deal with the fact that Paul probably had gotten that money from illegal means. He'd gotten in with a bad crop of people. Bran sat behind the wheel and thought about it. Then he had an idea.

Two hours later, he was back. He'd had the car stripped for parts by a friend who owned a salvage place. Michael gave him a thousand dollars for the parts, not a great deal, but that was okay. Bran, in turn, gave the money to an association for murder victims. The body of Paul's car was now being crushed on a heap of metal. It was the end. A sad end.

There were some delicious smells coming from the kitchen as he walked into the house. Carter had outdone himself. He'd made replicas of some of the most decadent and expensive desserts available.

"This is not Noka chocolate cake," he said, "but with a few ingredients added to fine chocolate, even the connoisseur wouldn't be able to tell the difference. Here, I've made a sample one to try." Carter held out a forkful of cake.

Bran closed his eyes as he tasted it. Noka chocolate retailed at eight hundred dollars or so a pound. It was known worldwide as the finest, most delicious chocolate, a combination of chocolates from Ecuador and Trinidad, merged to make a dark indulgence of over at least seventy-five percent chocolate.

"Sinful," he sighed.

"Next," Carter said. He showed Bran the perfect replica of the Golden Opulence Sundae, served in a restaurant in New York City at one thousand dollars a pop. Known as the world's most expensive sundae, the Golden Opulence was made with five scoops of Tahitian Vanilla Bean ice cream mixed with Madagascar vanilla and Venezuelan Chuao chocolate and topped off with a leaf covered in twenty-three-carat edible gold.

"It's not really gold." Carter smiled.

Bran laughed as he took a spoonful, tasting candied fruits, marzipan, and truffles. "Oh, God."

"It's drizzled with Amedie Porcelana chocolate," Carter added, "and topped with a Ron Ben-Israel sugar flower. I've replicated Amedie Porcelana. It's not exactly right, but close enough. On top of the sundae, you'll also find a small glass bowl of Grand Passion Caviar, sweetened with orange, passion fruit, and Armagnac, which gives off a shiny golden color. That I'm so proud of."

"You're a god," Bran told him.

Rick walked in. "Oh, you've been tasting the delights I see." He gave Bran a hug.

"He's a genius."

"And finally over here," Carter led them to the end of the counter, "I've done macaroons. They are simply two meringue puffs that are held together with buttercream. They are most popular in France, and you can usually find them for a reasonable price. However, I've tried to duplicate the macaroons of French pastry chef, Pierre Herme. He came up with a variety of tastes and flavors from peanut butter to balsamic vinegar. I hoped you're pleased."

"This is wonderful," Rick said. "Be sure and provide the information about these treats. The clients will be interested I'm sure."

Bran turned to Rick and kissed him. "It's all working out."

"Everything is on target for tonight. And I've increased our list of clientele by eight members."

Bran kissed him again. Of course, he would have gone right on kissing him if they'd been alone. They weren't. He did steer Rick aside and tell him the news about selling the shoes and how that would give them the push they needed to stay in the management game.

Rick smiled. "It was meant to be I guess."

"As we were." Bran smiled. *How can I feel this way about someone I just met? I just know. And when you know, as my dad always says, you know.*

They were interrupted by Finn just as Rick was about to kiss him.

"Bran, you're wanted."

Bran grunted in irritation and turned to look at Finn. "What is it?"

"Mr. Toshiri is back."

Bran closed his eyes. "Oh no. I promised him another . . . well . . ."

Rick smiled. "It's okay. Go ahead. I know it's only nibbling."

Bran laughed. "Last time. I know what I'm going to do. I'm going to borrow a stripper, give him two for one and then next time, he'll be into the other guy."

Both Finn and Rick nodded. "Good plan."

"Take Jake," Rick suggested. Mr. Toshiri likes them pale."

Bran made a face. "Okay, let's get this show on the road."

Bran was surprised at how delighted Mr. Toshiri was at the presentation both Bran and Jake made. He took to Jake like a fish to water, so to speak, and afterward, on the way back to the main room, Bran suggested that Jake be the man's main meal next time.

"You're in love," Mr. Toshiri commented, his gaze travelling to Rick, who was talking to a new client, getting him to fill out a survey. The man was short and stout, and Bran refrained from thinking about that song . . . something about a teapot. He shook himself. "How did you know?" he asked, smiling.

"It's in your face when you look at him," he replied, smiling over at Rick. "He is delicious."

Bran steered Mr. Toshiri to a comfortable chair. "And off limits," he told him, motioning to one of the pretty boys. "This, however, is for your pleasure."

Mr. Toshiri was captivated when the shiny, built, naked dancer straddled Mr. Toshiri and asked him quite seductively what he could get him for dessert.

Bran nodded and glanced around him. Clients were gobbling up Carter's imitations, fascinated with how exclusive these dishes were as the staff told stories about their origin. They were feeling privileged and pampered. And, judging by the cries from the dungeon, the clients downstairs were feeling just as exclusive.

In the kitchen, Rick grabbed him from behind and kissed his ear. "Happy?" he asked.

Rick turned around and smiled. "Delirious." He licked his lips. "You know, as long as we are together, I could get off on participating once in a while."

Rick eyed him. "Really?"

"Well." He looked at the floor, "we had fun downstairs."

He nodded.

"How about if we do Jack tomorrow night, the two of us? Brenda will be eating out of our hands, and she knows people."

Rick kissed Bran and winked. "I'm game. He wants to play straight boy controlled by two ravenous gay men."

"You got it."

"Fun!" Rick laughed. "That new man, he's a multi-millionaire. He tells me he doesn't know what to spend his money on."

"Perfect. What does he like?"

"He's a Dom, wants to play in the dungeon. He's got his sights on Teddy. Teddy is going to feed him macaroons."

Bran laughed. "Nothing like macaroons, with a side of whip and whipped cream."

The night passed quickly, and Waldo even showed up, which put Finn in an excellent mood. When the house was quiet, Bran and Rick crawled into bed together but were too tired for anything but some hot kisses. That was okay. They awoke early and made up for it. Rick rode him once on the bed and another time in the shower. It was heaven.

Waldo and Finn were smooching at the kitchen counter when Rick and Bran came down for breakfast. It was nice. They all drank coffee and Rick announced that he and Bran were taking care of Jack tonight.

Finn's eyes widened.

"Look," Bran said, "its fun for us to do it together."

Rick looked at Waldo. "Try it out sometime, with Finn. You'd be surprised what it does for your sex life."

"Would you . . . ah like to?" Finn raised an eyebrow.

"Maybe," Waldo nodded. "Wouldn't mind a threesome with one of those guys Rick hired."

Finn punched him.

They all laughed.

Rick motioned to Bran after they ate breakfast. "Come downstairs."

"What?"

"We have our costumes."

In the dungeon, Rick opened a bag. "Take a look."

"Holy!" Bran laughed. Black leather pants with the crotch and ass exposed and a black leather vest with laces to tie it. There was even a mask.

Rick ran his hand over the leather in Bran's hand. "I'm hard thinking of you dressed in that. Wait until you see the boots."

Bran followed Rick over to another box. He laughed. "My God." The boots were knee-high, laced all the way up with like four-inch heels. "Don't tell me I have to walk far in those?"

"No, honey." Rick pulled Bran into his arms. They began to kiss slowly, and Rick pushed Bran back a few steps. He lifted one of Bran's arms and caught his wrist in the strap, then did the same with the other and quickly fastened it.

Bran licked his lips and sucked in some air. "What are you going to do to me?"

Rick circled him like a shark. "I'm going to strip off your clothes," he breathed against his ear, "and take my time looking at you naked. Then I'm going to touch and fondle you everywhere, get out the play toys and plug every orifice and you're going to get a sound fucking while I fondle your cock and your balls at my leisure. I can't wait to play in your ass."

Bran was leaking come already, his cock swelling as Rick continued to talk. When his fingers slowly undid one button on his shirt after another, Bran moaned softly. One of Rick's fingertips touched his left nipple then circled it slowly. He pulled it out and twisted, leaving Bran breathless. A tongue touched it, laved it and teeth yanked on it. Bran's head went back as again Rick pinched the same nipple then clamped something on it.

Bran grunted. "Ooh . . . yeah."

Rick circled the same nipple, playing with the clamp, tugging on it. He didn't touch the other nipple, which felt like it was begging for attention. Rick's palms slid over Bran's stomach to his jeans. He rubbed his knuckles over the zipper then slid it down. Roughly, he exposed Bran's cock and let it hang out of his briefs. He didn't touch him. Instead, Rick said, "I'm looking at your cock, so hard, so sensitive. I think it needs discipline."

Bran licked his lips. He didn't fear Rick. He'd never hurt him, but a little sting increased pleasure and Rick was an expert. Fingers pinched the tip of his cock, then cuffed it back and forth. Bran let out a cry. "Please."

His cock was lifted and strapped. "So nice on display. Mine."

"Yes, yours baby," Bran groaned.

Rick came around back and pulled down his pants and underwear. He massaged his ass cheeks and then gave them a smack.

Bran laughed. "I've been bad."

"So bad." Rick kissed his neck.

Bran heard the sound of Rick's zipper coming down then felt his erection against Bran's ass. He teased him for a few minutes then separated his ass cheeks and inserted a slippery plug. "Oh God," Bran grunted.

"Feel filled, baby?" Rick moved his cock against Bran's ass.

"It's succulent pleasure."

Rick came around to suck on the unclamped nipple while he played with the other. A little tug and the sensation went straight to Bran's cock. "Ooooh."

Rick fondled Bran's balls and his strapped cock. "I'm going to use the lightest of whips on those nipples and cock. Won't make a mark but you'll feel it."

Bran braced himself for the sensation. Rick pulled off the clamp. Bran bit his bottom lip, then Rick swung the whip. The sensation of soft bristles touching his skin was incredible. It stiffened his sensitive nipples and tormented his cock. Rick moved around back. He pushed a small stool under him. "Get up on that and bend forward. Legs far apart, baby."

Bran stepped on the small bench, and Rick let the soft whip go between Rick's ass cheeks, hitting the end of the plug. If he hadn't been strapped, he would have come big time.

Rick walked around and undid the strap then went to the back again. He pulled out the plug and let the whip slid between Bran's ass cheeks. Bran came so hard he let out a scream.

Rick pulled him off the stool and grabbed his hips. He

pushed his cock into his ass slowly, then as deep as he could, not thrusting until he was in all the way. Bran felt such sublime pleasure, and Rick reached around and stroked Bran back to life as he began to thrust faster and harder.

One hand rubbed his nipples voraciously, and the other jerked his cock, played with his balls, as Rick's beautiful big cock filled his ass. Bran came again just before Rick did, his body undulating as Rick continued to run his hands all over him. "Oh God, I feel like such a slut."

"My slut," Rick grunted, undoing his hands and pulling him around into his arms for passionate kisses.

Bran chuckled. "My kinky boyfriend," he murmured, kissing him with gusto.

"You're naked."

Both Bran and Rick turned to see Finn standing there.

Rick zipped up his pants and grinned. Bran scrambled to pick up his underwear and jeans. "We were ah . . . practicing."

"I see that," Finn muttered, trying to keep a straight face. "I think you've had enough practice now?"

Rick cleared his throat. "Was just leaving to get a . . . something." He lowered his head and ran up the stairs.

Bran burst out laughing.

Finn came over and hugged him. "I'm happy for you."

"And Waldo?"

"He's warming up."

It was just the two of them suddenly, he and Finn. They'd been through so much together, had come close to being a couple, then for some reason, they didn't. But that was okay. Bran moved closer. "You know I'll always love you no matter what."

Finn nodded. "Me, too." He linked his arm with Bran. "Now let's get ready for tonight. We have a lot to do. And aren't you in the spotlight?"

"This is the last time though," Bran said seriously.

"Tell me another one," Finn threw at him. They looked at each other and laughed as Finn linked his arm with Bran. After a brief hug, they separated and raced each other up the stairs.

About the Authors

A.J. Llewellyn is the author of over 250 M/M romance novels. She was born in Australia, and lives in Los Angeles. An early obsession with Robinson Crusoe led to a lifelong love affair with islands, particularly Hawaii and Easter Island.

Being marooned once on Wedding Cake Island in Australia cured her of a passion for fishing, but led to a plotline for a novel. A.J.'s friends live in fear because even the smallest details of their lives usually wind up in her stories. A.J. has a desire to paint, draw, juggle, work for the FBI, walk a tightrope with an elephant, be a chess champion, a steeplejack, master chef, and a world-class surfer. She can't do any of these things so she writes about them instead.

A.J. started life as a journalist and boxing columnist, and still enjoys interrogating, er, interviewing people to find out what makes them tick.

How to find/friend me:

email: ajllewellyn@gmail.com
website: www.ajllewellyn.com
www.facebook.com/aj.llewellyn
www.twitter.com/ajllewellyn
Newsletter sign-up: ajllewellynnewsletter@gmail.com — each month I give away a free ebook!

I'm an app! Download my FREE A.J. Llewellyn App for Android here: http://tinyurl.com/lkbc4wm

D.J. Manly

I write not only for my own pleasure, but for the pleasure of my readers. I can't remember a time in my life when I haven't written and told stories. When I'm not writing, I'm dreaming about writing, doing something wild and adventurous, or trying to make the world a better and more open minded place to live in. I adore beautiful men, and I know I'm not alone in this! Eroticism between consenting adults, in all its many forms is the icing on the cake of life!

D.J. has published well over two hundred novels/novella's, and is a well seasoned writer.

9 781487 424602